倒掉水

Spilled Water

Sally Grindley

BLOOMSBURY

Published by Bloomsbury, New York and London
Distributed to the trade by Holtzbrinck Publishers

Library of Congress Cataloging-in-Publication Data
Grindley, Sally.
Spilled water / by Sally Grindley.
p. cm.
Summary: After her father's death, Lu Si-yan's uncle sells her to a rich family who expects her to work as their servant until she is old enough to marry their son, but when she runs away things only get worse.
ISBN 1-58234-937-1 (alk. paper)
[1. Household employees—Fiction. 2. Factories—Fiction. 3. Family life—China—Fiction. 4. Arranged marriage—China—Fiction. 5. China—Fiction.]
I. Title.
PZ7.G88446Sp 2004
[Fic]—dc22
2003065816

First U.S. Edition 2004
Printed in Great Britain by Clays Ltd, St Ives plc
1 3 5 7 9 10 8 6 4 2

Bloomsbury USA Children's Books
175 Fifth Avenue
New York, NY 10010

All papers used by Bloomsbury Publishing are natural, recyclable products made from wood grown in well-managed forests. The manufacturing processes conform to the environmental regulations of the country of origin.

For Alan, with love

Chapter One

To Market

I loved my baby brother, until Uncle took me to market and sold me. He was the bright, shiny pebble in the water, the twinkling star in the sky. Until Uncle took me to market and sold me. Then I hated him.

'Lu Si-yan,' Uncle greeted me early one summer morning, 'today is a big day for you. From today, you must learn to find your own way in the muddy whirlpool of life. Your mother and I have given you a good start. Now it is your turn.'

My mother stood in the shadows of our kitchen, but she didn't look at me and she didn't say a word. Uncle took me tightly by the wrist. As he led me from the house, my mother reached out her hand towards me and clawed the air as though trying to pull me back. Then she picked up my little brother and hid behind the door, but I saw her face wither with pain and, in that moment, fear gripped my heart.

'Where are you taking me, Uncle Ba?' I cried.

'It's for the best,' he replied, his mouth set grimly.

'You're hurting my arm,' I cried.

He pulled me past the scorched patchwork terraces of my family's smallholding, scattering hens and ducks along the way, and out on to the dusty track that led steeply up to the road. There, we walked, Uncle brisk and businesslike, me dragging my feet in protest, until we came to the bus-stop.

'Where are we going, Uncle Ba?' I whimpered this time.

'To market,' he said.

'What are we going to buy?' I asked.

Chapter Two

The Happiest Soul
on Earth

Everybody loved my father. My mother used to say that
he was the happiest soul on earth. When you were with
him he made you feel happy too.

When there was just me, he used to lift me on to his
shoulders and gallop down to the river, where he picked
me up by the armpits and dangled my feet in the water. I
screamed at the cold, but then he put my feet in his
jacket pockets, one in each side, and we galloped off
again, laughing all the way.

When there was just me, he sat me in his rickshaw
and cycled along the road, weaving from one side to the
other, bump, bump, bump across the cobbles, singing at
the top of his voice. I lurched up and down on the seat,

yelling at him to stop but wanting him to carry on.

When there was just me, he taught me to play chess and wei-qi, and sometimes I won, but I knew that he was letting me. We played mahjong with Uncle and my mother. Father and I made silly bird noises every time it came to the 'twittering of the sparrows', while Uncle tutted and my mother rolled her eyes heavenwards in mock exasperation.

We never had much money, but I didn't really notice because neither did anyone else in our village. Father's favourite saying was, 'If you realise that you have enough, you are truly rich', and he believed it. 'We have fresh food and warm clothes, a roof over our heads (a bit leaky when it rains) and a wooden bed to sleep on. What more can we ask for?' he demanded. 'And not only that,' he continued, 'but I have the finest little dumpling of a daughter in the whole of China.'

My parents worked hard to make sure that we always had enough. Father set off early in the morning, his farming tools over his shoulder, to tend the dozens of tiny terraces of vegetables that straggled higgledy-piggledy over the hillside above and below our house. He dug and sowed and weeded and cropped throughout the numbing cold of winter and the suffocating heat of summer. In the middle of the day, he returned home clutching triumphantly a gigantic sheaf of pakchoi, a basin of bright green beans, or a bucket full of melon-sized turnips.

'Your father can grow the biggest, tastiest vegetables on a piece of land the size of a silk handkerchief,' Mother used to say, and I would skip off to help him because I wanted one day to grow the biggest, tastiest vegetables as well.

Mostly, I spent the mornings with Mother, feeding the hens and ducks and collecting their eggs which were scattered around our yard. There were slops to be taken out to our pig and fresh straw to be laid. Once a week, along with our neighbours and their children, we carried our clothes down to the river to wash them. That was the best day. When it was hot, we children pulled off the clothes we were wearing and charged into the river, splashing wildly and shrieking our heads off. We learnt to swim very young and raced backwards and forwards through the sparkling waters. As soon as we were back on the shore, our mothers attacked us with soap, then we dashed into the water again to rinse it off, before running around in the sun to dry. In winter, the river sometimes froze for days on end. Some of the older children went skating on it, but Father said they were foolish because they might fall in.

Mother was ready with soup and rice when my father returned at midday. He used to sit me on his knee and ask me what I had been up to all morning. I made up stories about fighting dragons and escaping from haunted temples and he would sit there saying, 'Did you? Did you really? What a morning that must have been!' until we dissolved into fits of giggles and Father said, 'I hope the rest of the day will be quieter for you.'

In the afternoons, Father returned to his terraces, or he would walk several miles with other villagers to work on the rice fields that they shared. Mother went to the village to shop and to gossip, and I went with her to play with my friends. Nobody minded us dashing in and out of the shops in a boisterous game of hide-and-seek, and the old men smiled as we peered over their shoulders to watch them playing cards on wobbly foldaway tables in the street.

Back home again, Mother and I prepared the evening meal, ready for my father's return. Sometimes, if he was early enough, he took his boat out on the river to fish.

He would let me go with him if I promised to be ever so quiet. Once we caught the biggest carp anyone in the village had ever seen. If we stood it on its tail it was taller than me! We took it to market and sold it for so much money that Father was able to buy us each a new pair of shoes.

Father never worked on Sunday afternoons. If necessary, he worked still harder during the week in order to free himself for his 'family time'. On Sundays, he sharpened all our kitchen knives, selected the very best vegetables from our farm, killed one of our chickens, and set to work with spices and herbs and ginger and garlic in preparation for our evening meal. This was his favourite time. We would sit at the table and talk to him as he chopped away. We were not allowed to help.

'You have had to prepare my meals all week,' he would say to my mother. 'Now it is my turn to prepare your meal.'

If ever Mother argued that he had been working all week long on the farm and should put his feet up, he simply said, 'That is different, and in any case I enjoy cooking. I want to cook, and I want you to put your feet up.'

Mother grumbled good-humouredly at his stubborn-
ness, but we knew that he loved every minute of his
weekly role as chef. And he was good at it. The meals
we ate on Sunday evenings were the best, Mother was
happy to admit it. When they were over, we sat down as
a family and watched television. It didn't matter what
was on – it was just the being there together that we
loved.

Chapter Three
To Market

Uncle remained silent, sucking hard on a cigarette, leaving my question hanging in the heavy morning air, until a bus came along and he pushed me aboard. Two women I recognised from a nearby village were already sitting inside. They immediately asked us where we were going. Uncle said a name that meant nothing to me, while making it clear that he did not wish to discuss his business any further. I heard one of the women whisper that, my goodness, we were going on a long journey, and the two of them wondered aloud what on earth we might be going all that way for. Uncle ignored them, while I tried to make sense of the disturbing turn of events that had thrown my life into confusion.

I gazed out of the window, slightly comforted to realise that the landscape was still familiar. Father and I had come this far many a time in the past, bump, bump, bump in his rickshaw. Then the bus stopped and the two women clambered off, waving goodbye to me, wishing me a pleasant journey. They headed in the direction of a street lined with colourful stalls. I saw that it was the market where my father always used to sell his vegetables and where we had sold his enormous carp.

'Why aren't we going to that market?' I asked.

'Too small,' said Uncle brusquely.

The bus rumbled on again, leaving the world I knew behind it, to climb, twist, speed through countryside, villages and towns I had never seen before. Gradually the motion of the bus sent me to sleep.

I woke up to find myself stretched out across Uncle's lap, his arm curled round my shoulder. When he saw that I was awake, he pulled his arm away abruptly, as though he didn't want me to think that he was showing any affection for me. I sat up and looked around. The bus was empty apart from us. Outside, it was growing dark. How many hours had we been travelling? We'd left home soon after breakfast. We'd had nothing to eat since. I was ravenous.

'How much further?' I said. 'I'm starving.'

'Not long,' said Uncle. He reached in his pocket and gave me a piece of cake which my mother must have baked.

'When are we going home again?' I asked.

Chapter Four

Your Heart is Filled
with Stone

Uncle Ba was my father's brother. He was ten years older than my father. He had helped their mother to bring up my father when their father had died. I didn't like Uncle much. I thought he was bossy, and he didn't smile very often. He was always interfering in our lives, telling Father that he should go and work in a factory to earn more money, that he spoilt me, that I should go to a minder so that Mother could find work.

Father would chuckle and say, 'Your heart is filled with stone, my brother,' but I knew that he was bruised by such words of disapproval from someone he loved. I once overheard him tell my mother that Uncle had been the most devoted brother to him when they had grown up together, and that he would forgive my uncle anything. He admitted, however, that Uncle had changed since wealth and position had come his way.

Uncle Ba lived in a large house on the other side of the village, though we were never invited to visit. He caught a bus every day to travel to a factory two hours away. He had been a farmer like my father, but had been delighted to give up such gruelling work. He had never married. He used to say that he felt himself incapable of devoting enough time, energy and affection to one person to make them happy, especially having spent so many years looking after my father. Once, when Father wasn't listening, Mother said that Uncle had become far too selfish to invite anyone into his life and how fortunate that was for womankind.

Uncle was family, though, and family was important. Both my father's parents were now dead, as were my grandparents on my mother's side. Father would do anything for his brother, and regularly took him the pick of his vegetables and his prize catch of fish. He invited him to eat with us at least four times a week, even when we were short of food for ourselves. Uncle would sit there telling us about his new life and how much money he was making, how respected he was now and how he expected one day to be able to run his own business.

'Just think, brother,' he would often say, 'if you were like me, you would be able to dress your wife in fine clothes, and she would be able to serve up a meal fit for an emperor instead of a pauper.'

Mother would bridle with anger and reply, 'He is not like you, and I have no desire for fine clothes.'

'Nonsense,' Uncle would insist. 'Every woman yearns for fine clothes.'

'We are happy as we are,' Father would say quietly. 'People are all different in their needs.'

Mostly, Uncle ignored me, except to criticise my table manners, or my behaviour, or, being a female child, the burden I imposed upon my family. I didn't understand what he meant by that at the time, but I knew that he didn't think much of me. Once, when Uncle spent a whole evening telling me not to put my head in my food, not to lick my chopsticks, not to jig up and down, not to hum, not to speak unless I was spoken to, I kicked him under the table, hard on the shin, and pretended it was an accident. He didn't believe me and demanded that I be sent out of the room. My parents resisted, certain that I would never do such a thing on purpose, and I stayed. Uncle went home, furious. I was triumphant. Father looked at me and said, 'I hope you didn't kick your uncle on purpose,' then he winked and turned away without another word.

Chapter Five

A Silk Swallow and a Handsome Tiger

I was six when my baby brother was born. I remember Mother disappearing into the bedroom and Father boiling water in a pan and fetching clean cloths. I remember women from the village arriving and lots of hushed whispers and one of them sat me on her knee. I remember my mother screaming and my father, ashen-faced, telling me not to worry. I remember a small strangled cry and the village women cheering and my father hugging me and hugging me. I remember going into the bedroom with him and feeling his boundless joy and seeing my mother, her black hair damp with perspiration, holding the tiniest little baby I had ever seen. I remember my mother saying, 'You've got a little brother,

Si-yan. Isn't he beautiful?', and I remember holding his tiny hand and thinking I was the luckiest girl in the whole of China to have such a beautiful baby brother.

Uncle Ba arrived just then and congratulated my parents loudly, before muttering quietly to my father – but I heard him – 'Your wife got it right this time, at least, but there can be no more.'

A shadow of anguish fell across my father's face of joy. I tried to puzzle out what my Uncle meant, as he brushed past me, demanding to hold my little brother. Then I wanted to stop him because I didn't want him to go anywhere near.

'He's not yours, leave him alone!' I heard myself cry.

My father knelt down and held me close.

'It's all right, my little swallow,' he soothed. 'Uncle Ba won't harm him.'

I watched, ball-fisted, as Uncle picked up my little brother and rocked him in his arms. I saw his face soften and his eyes grow moist. I wished I knew what I had done to upset him that he couldn't be like that with me. When Uncle had put my brother down again, he turned to my father and said, 'Another mouth to feed, how will you manage?'

My father gripped my shoulder. 'We'll manage,' he said, 'just as we always have.'

Uncle Ba raised his eyebrows.

'You may have to change your mind about that factory job,' he warned.

'I don't think so,' replied my father.

When Uncle Ba had gone, my mother fell asleep. Father picked up my little brother and laid him in my arms. I gazed down at his apple cheeks and shock of black hair, the way his eyelids quivered and his lips sucked together. I loved him there and then, wanting him to open his eyes, to look at me and love me too.

'Do you like the name "Li-hu", Si-yan?' asked my father. 'That's the name your mother and I are thinking about.'

'Lu Li-hu,' I tried out. 'Lu Si-yan and Lu Li-hu, Lu Si-yan and Lu Li-hu,' I sang. 'A silk swallow and a handsome tiger. I hope the tiger doesn't eat the poor swallow.'

'When he is old enough, my handsome tiger will protect and treasure my beautiful silk swallow,' laughed Father.

'Perhaps your silk swallow will protect and treasure

your handsome tiger,' I giggled.

Li-hu quickly flourished from a plump, gurgling, contented baby into a sturdy, boisterous toddler. I watched, entranced, as he fed from my mother, smiled his first smile, wriggled across the floor on his bottom, and took his first steps. I jiggled him up and down on my knee, pushed him in a wooden cart Father had made for me when I was little, helped him to eat his first proper meals, and sang lullabies to him at bedtime.

When Father played the same games with Li-hu as he had played with me, sometimes I minded a bit, sometimes I felt jealous, but most of the time I watched and laughed and urged him on. If Father wasn't there, I played the same games and took his role, grown-up as anything. Father and I still had our own special moments, especially after Li-hu had gone to bed, doing things that my little brother was too young to join in with or understand. Father said I was his big girl now, which made me feel very important.

I started to go to the village school. Father wanted me to learn to read and write, and one day to go to university.

'You shall have every advantage that we didn't have,'

he declared. 'Anyone who still thinks that women have no need for education is living in the dark ages. Go and learn and make me proud.'

I worked hard at my lessons, for I wanted to make Father proud. I came home each evening and we sat down and he would ask me what I had learnt that day. It was only as I began to be able to read and write, and Father questioned me in detail about particular words, studying their shape and the way different strokes were added, that I realised he could barely read and write himself. Then he became my pupil and I loved teaching him.

Uncle called him an old fool for even thinking that he could learn at his age, especially from me.

'It's a waste of what precious little money you have, sending this girl-child to school,' he tutted, 'and it's a bigger waste of your precious time to sit with her believing she can teach you anything but nonsense.'

'The journey of a thousand miles starts from beneath your feet,' Father quoted, and, though I struggled to understand what he meant, I could see from the brightness of his eyes that our lessons touched his soul.

'Your father is like a young child with a new toy,'

Mother smiled.

'This young child will never grow tired of his new toy,' Father laughed back.

He was right. He didn't grow tired of it. He didn't have the chance to. Father died, and the sun went out of our lives.

Chapter Six
To Market

'Questions, always questions,' muttered Uncle Ba.

Before I could pursue my question, and I was determined he should answer me, a boy pulled out on his bicycle right in front of the bus. The bus driver stamped hard on his brakes, throwing us out of our seats. The bus screeched and shuddered to a halt inches from the cyclist. Then the driver opened his window and let out a torrent of abuse, accompanied by a pantomime of rude gestures, as the boy recovered his bicycle and disappeared down a dusty track. Uncle shouted something about 'stupid simpletons'. For the next few minutes he and the driver engaged in a loud exchange about the stupidity of peasant farmers and their offspring.

From my window I saw that we were leaving behind a barren stretch of rocky countryside to enter a colourless old town. Steep and winding alleyways spidered off from the road above and below us, crammed all along with dilapidated wooden shacks. These gave way to grey apartment blocks, their balconies hung with washing, dried meats and plaits of garlic, and so close together that their occupants could shake hands across the passages in between. The road was now lined with shopfronts, their goods spilling out on to the pavements, where chickens pecked at anything they could find and dogs ran wild. A little boy waved at me as we went by, and I wanted so much to be back with Li-hu and Mother.

I was about to ask Uncle again when we would be going home, when I suddenly noticed that a number of young girls were walking all in the same direction, up the road. Several of them were on their own, but others were holding hands with men whom I assumed to be their fathers. They all looked thoroughly miserable. Where were they going? I wondered. Why were they so unhappy?

The bus drew level with a girl of about thirteen. She was two or three paces behind a man and was looking nervously around her. Just at that moment, she threw her bag to the ground, turned and ran off down the road. I stood up to watch as the man she was with tore after her. He caught up with her and slapped her hard round the face, before dragging her back up the road. I was so shocked that I slumped back into my seat and burst into tears.

'I want to go home,' I spluttered. 'Please let me go home.'

'It's too late, I'm afraid,' replied Uncle quietly. 'We're here now.'

Chapter Seven

All You Have is What You Grow

I was nine when my father died. It was very sudden. One day he was there, the next day he wasn't. Mother didn't tell me very much. She couldn't. She hugged me and she hugged Li-hu and we hugged each other and cried together, hour after hour, but she couldn't speak. I don't think she could bring herself to say the words that bore the truth of what had happened – words that meant that Father was never coming back.

Uncle Ba said that my father had been hit by a taxi which had swerved to miss a child. He had died almost instantly and wouldn't have felt much pain. He had begged the people who tended him to ask Uncle to look after us. He had left us his undying love.

For days afterwards, our friends from the village visited us to offer their sympathy and support. They made tea, brought us meals, washed our clothes and worked on the farm. Mother seemed to perk up while they were around, but, after a week, Uncle asked them to stay away, saying that we had to learn to fend for ourselves and that the time for mourning was over. He told my mother that she must be strong for her children. He told me that until my brother was old enough I must take on my father's role. We weren't ready, though. Our grief was too crippling.

Everything reminded me of Father. His old rickshaw sat rusting in the yard. No more bump, bump, bump, but Mother couldn't bear to part with it. His jacket hung by the door as though waiting for him to struggle into it, just as he had every morning after breakfast. Our mahjong set sat on a shelf gathering dust. Li-hu kept asking when Father was coming home. He was too young to understand.

I tried. I tried so hard. I took Li-hu with me to help feed the ducks and hens, and turned collecting their eggs into a game. I carried slops out to the pig and spread clean straw across the yard. I loaded Li-hu's wooden cart with some of the turnips Father had stored in his shed and pushed it to the village, Li-hu riding on top. I exchanged the turnips for rice or tea or noodles. Back home again, I prepared our meals and tried to make Mother eat. She sat in a chair, gazing out of the window down towards the river, scarcely saying a word. Li-hu clambered on and off her lap over and over again. She would stroke his hair, he would suck his thumb, but she wasn't able to give him the comfort he needed, so he would pull himself abruptly away and demand my lap instead. We would snuggle up together and he would ask me when Mother would stop being sad. For a while I felt that I had lost not only my father but my mother too, and I felt the chill of suddenly being all alone.

Uncle kept away during those early days. I was glad because I didn't want to hear him say anything bad about my mother.

He arrived one evening, unannounced, and claimed that business matters had taken up his time, and that in any case we couldn't expect to rely upon him.

He walked all over Father's terraces, then sat down to eat with us.

'How are you going to survive?' he asked bluntly at

31

last, cutting through the silence that had even claimed my brother with its awkwardness.

Mother shifted uncomfortably on her chair, her meal untouched before her.

'All you have is what you grow,' Uncle continued, 'and yet already you are neglecting your lifeline, the lifeline my brother left you. How can you dishonour his memory in this way?'

I watched the despair spread across my mother's face.

'And look at you, sister,' he said more gently, but his words were harsher. 'Look at your shrunken body. Look at your dirty clothes. Look at your filthy house. Look at your ragamuffin children. When are you going to come to your senses?'

I couldn't bear it any longer. 'Leave us alone!' I shouted. 'We're doing our best. Can't you see we're doing our best?'

'Then your best isn't good enough, madam,' retorted Uncle. He stood up from the table and walked out of the house.

When he had gone, Li-hu crawled on to my lap, thumb in mouth. I sat for some time, my thoughts too wretched to air. Then Mother rose, as though from a dream, put her arm round my shoulder and kissed me gently on the forehead.

'Why does Uncle Ba have to be so cruel?' I asked.

'Your uncle is hurting, Si-yan,' my mother replied. 'For all his harsh words, he loved your father and misses him terribly. They went through so much together when they were young.'

I was astonished at what she said. If Uncle loved my father, he had a curious way of showing it.

'And perhaps your uncle is being cruel to be kind,' she added. 'He is right. I must pull myself together, for all our sakes.'

I threw my arms round her waist, happy that at last my mother had come back to me.

'Thank you, Si-yan, thank you for keeping things going,' she said then. 'We'll do this together from now on, you and me and little Li-hu. No more tears. We'll make your father proud of us.'

She picked up Li-hu, kissed his fat cheeks and squeezed him tight. Li-hu hugged her back, making up for the days when she had neglected him. He refused to let go until I put on Father's jacket and gave him a pocket ride round and round the yard.

Chapter Eight
To Market

The bus stopped a little way before a narrow bridge.

'This is as far as I go,' the driver addressed my uncle.

Uncle nodded, took my arm, and led me along the gangway.

'Spilled water, is she?' asked the driver.

Uncle didn't answer, just pulled me down the steps.

'I thought so,' said the driver. 'A lot of them are who come here. Yours is younger than most, mind.'

Uncle tried to pull me out of earshot as the driver, warming to his subject, called after him, 'It's illegal, you know,' followed by a dismissive, 'but nobody seems to do anything about it.'

Uncle hurried me across the bridge. I was petrified. I didn't know what the driver had meant, but I knew instinctively that it was bad.

'Where are you taking me?' I demanded, sensing that this was my last chance to gain control of what was happening to me. 'I won't go. You can't make me go.'

'It's for the sake of your mother and your brother,' was all Uncle would say. 'You wouldn't want them to suffer, would you?'

'Of course I wouldn't, but tell me, why can't you just tell me?'

Ahead of me, set back from the road against a backdrop of granite cliffs, at the end of a rough track, I saw a huge, wooden, barn-like building. Parked outside were large numbers of vans, rickshaws, motorised carts and several taxis. Muffled shouts came from inside the building.

Uncle turned up the track. I stopped where I was.

'I'm not going any further until you tell me, Uncle.'

'And what do you think you're going to do otherwise, madam?' he snapped. 'Your mother can't afford to keep you and your brother, so you have to go. Your brother is more important. It is he who will continue your father's name and, when he is old enough, he will work to keep your mother and to pay back the ever-increasing debt she owes me. What little money you fetch here will also go towards paying back your mother's debts. Is that what you wanted to hear?'

Suddenly, he looked horrified by the sound of his own words. He closed his eyes, bit his lip, then tried to put a hand on my shoulder. I shrank away from him, unable to take in what he meant.

'There's no end to it otherwise, don't you see?' He seemed almost to beg my understanding. 'No end to it.'

Chapter Nine
Doing Our Best

It was so good to have Mother back. We became an inseparable team. We attacked life wholeheartedly, determined that together we could cope with anything. Mother didn't say it, but I knew that she was driven by a need to prove Uncle wrong, while the memory of my father kept us going when our spirits flagged.

We would work from the moment day broke until the dense dark of night. No challenge was too overwhelming for us. We set to work straightaway on Father's terraces, making up for the weeks of neglect with the most painstaking weeding and watering. We were rewarded when the rows of wilted pakchoi and cabbage revived and flourished in the warm sunshine.

We gave Li-hu the job of feeding the hens and ducks and collecting their eggs. He loved it, especially chasing them away from where they were sitting in case there was an egg hidden underneath them. We giggled at his shrieks of laughter while we tidied the house and prepared our lunch.

On washing days, while Mother went down to the river, I walked into the village with Li-hu, pushing him in his cart, to do the shopping. Sometimes the shopkeepers would give us a piece of meat or fish, or an extra portion of noodles.

'Take it,' they would say. 'We know how hard it is for you and you deserve a little help.'

Others would come up to us and tell us how much they missed my father and what a wonderful man he had been. It made me feel happy to know how much my father was loved. I always told Mother what had been said. She would nod and smile and her eyes would go all misty with pride and missing him.

Mother began to use Father's rickshaw. We filled it once a week with all our freshly-picked vegetables and rode to the market in the next town, not bumping, but singing loudly all the songs that Father used to sing. We left Li-hu back in the village with friends, and these were the times I relished the most, just being with my mother and being a team and doing our best, which was good enough.

What saddened me the most was that I could no longer go to school. We couldn't afford it any more, and there was too much else to do with helping my mother and looking after Li-hu. I didn't resent it, but I missed my friends. Once, though, I bumped into my teacher in the village. She gave me a book to read and said to take it back to her when I had finished it and she would lend me another one. Whenever I had a spare moment, I read that book. As soon as I had finished it, I collected another one. Reading became my escape. I loved losing myself in adventure stories, away from the harsh demands of the adult world into which I had been plunged.

Uncle stopped by once a week. He looked more and more affluent, more and more aloof, as though we were rather inferior to him, and as though calling to see us was an irksome duty he was obliged to carry out in spite of himself. I thought he was like a spy, and I felt that he wanted us to fail, though I had no idea why. He would stride over Father's terraces, prodding the ground with a stick and bending down to inspect the undersides of our crops. He would poke around in the shed, counting the root vegetables we had stored there. He would walk round the yard, lifting the straw to see how fresh it was. Then he would go indoors and pass his hand over the table and chairs, checking for dirt.

Uncle still expected us to feed him when he visited, though he never brought anything to the meal. He seemed taken aback when we served him meat, and had to admit, grudgingly, that we were managing.

'Of course,' he said, 'it's early days yet. The weather has been kind. It won't be so easy for you when the weather changes.'

Not once did Uncle offer us any sort of help, and I began to wish that he would just stay away. If he wasn't a spy, I thought to myself, he was like a vulture waiting to pick over the bones of some poor dead animal.

Chapter Ten
Sold

I was so numbed by what Uncle had said that I did as I was told and followed him like a sheep up the track and into the barn. *'Your mother can't afford to keep you ... You have to go ... What little money you fetch ...'*

I don't know what I expected to find there, but nothing prepared me for the shouting and laughter, the stench of stale sweat and the clouds of cigarette smoke that assaulted me as we went through the doors. Uncle too looked taken aback, but he spoke rapidly to a man standing by the entrance and handed him some money.

Then he turned to me and said, 'We're here to find you a job. Take this notice and come with me.'

He gripped me by the elbow and led me across the room, through the hordes of men who were milling around. As we went by, they eyed me up and down with an improper interest which made me feel humiliated and uneasy.

Dozens of other young girls were standing on the other side of a rope, most of them at least three or four years older than me, some of them clutching scribbled notices, some with boards by their feet. I recognised the girl who had been slapped in the street. She was holding a notice which read: 'I am Jin Yanhua. I am 13. I can cook and I am very obedient.' She still bore the red marks across her cheek from the slap, and her eyes were wild with anguish. A man was leaning across the rope, lifting her hair, stroking her bare arm. She shook him off and the man who had slapped her said something to her angrily.

'Go behind the rope, Lu Si-yan,' Uncle said tersely, 'and please try to look agreeable.'

An old man stepped towards me and touched my face. I pulled away in disgust and ducked under the rope, happier to be amongst the other girls than with Uncle and the leering men who terrified me. I looked at the notice Uncle had given me. 'My name is Lu Si-yan,' it read. 'I am young but can wash, cook and sew. I will be a good servant.'

How could Uncle do this? How could he? Father had asked him to look after me, not to sell me, for I realised now that this was what was happening. Did Mother know just what he was planning? Could she have done anything to stop it? If only Li-hu hadn't been born, we would have managed, Mother and I. We would have done our best and managed. It was Li-hu's fault. As I stood there in my shame and humiliation, a tiny drop of spilled water, I hated my brother.

One after another, men called me forward to take a closer look at me, to inspect me, like some sort of item in a shop. Some of them pointed at me and laughed. Others talked to Uncle in hushed voices, but once I heard him say 'She is a very obedient girl' and another time I heard 'You won't find anyone better'.

A middle-aged man, short and fat, with dirty finger-nails and missing teeth, kept coming back to examine me. I was petrified that he was going to choose me, until Uncle sent him away, saying that he couldn't afford me.

Another middle-aged man became very agitated with Uncle. He pulled a wad of money from his pocket and waved it in front of Uncle's face, but Uncle shook his head dismissively and pushed the man's hand away. The man shoved Uncle in the chest, then spat on the ground and sputtered, 'Pah! Your puny little frog is not worth the money you ask. Take her back to your pond then, where she'll spawn a million more, all useless like herself.'

He marched off through the crowd. Uncle gazed at me awkwardly, then shrugged his shoulders and waited for the next approach.

By now I was faint with hunger. The smoke and noise and smells fanned a growing sense of unreality which took me far, far away from the room and off into a sunlit world, where Father was on the river in his boat and I was skipping along the shore waving to him. Suddenly, he caught an enormous fish. He hauled it into the boat, then held it up for me to see. 'We'll eat well tonight,' he said but, just as he said it, a dense mist came down and swirled around him. I cried out to him and I heard him calling my name, over and over again, but the mist simply swallowed him up as he stood there proudly holding his fish.

When the mist cleared, Uncle was shaking me by the shoulder, across the rope, and telling me to pick up my notice.

'Pull yourself together, child,' he hissed. 'No one will want you if you look ill.'

What if nobody did want me? I wondered. Would that mean I could go home? Would that mean the nightmare would be over? A flicker of hope dared to ignite within me, only to be extinguished instantly when a sombre, thin-faced man approached my uncle. He was well dressed in a smart suit, and seemed out of place among the noisy hordes. He was obviously impatient to conduct his business and leave. He stared hard at me, then asked Uncle several questions. I strained to hear what was said, but the man's voice was too low-pitched. Uncle was eager, though, I could see that.

While they continued to talk, I studied the man. He was taller than Uncle – thin, with pockmarked skin and big hands. What I noticed most was that his eyes were cold – empty and cold. They allowed not a hint of expression as he talked to Uncle, which made me shiver nervously. I had long been the target of Uncle's hostility and hard-heartedness and expected nothing different from him, but there was passion and anger in him as well. This man seemed to show no emotion of any sort.

The man reached into his pockets and took out what

looked like a photograph. Uncle studied it, then nodded approvingly, glancing sideways in my direction as he did so. The man pulled out his wallet and held out a roll of money. Uncle hesitated, before taking it quickly and putting it inside his coat. He shook hands with the man, then lifted up the rope and brought me over to his side.

'Lu Si-yan, this is Mr Chen. You will go with him. He is in charge of you now. Make sure you bring honour to your family by your good manners and behaviour.'

'I don't want to go, Uncle. Please don't make me go.'

I begged with him, pleaded with him. I thought for a moment that he might change his mind when his face seemed to soften and he gazed at me briefly with concern. But he dismissed me quickly with a pat on the shoulder, and marched away without looking back. My new owner signalled for me to go with him. I lowered my head, not to show obedience, but to hide my tears.

What was to become of me? I was eleven years old, far from my home, far from my family, in the hands of a stranger, and nobody cared. As I followed Mr Chen from the building, I was certain of only one thing: that no matter what happened, one day, one day soon, I would see my mother again.

A taxi was waiting outside. Mr Chen opened a door and sat next to me in the back. We drove for a few miles in silence, darkness descending all around us, then I fell asleep. I woke when the car stopped and he told me to get out. We turned into a building and waited for the lift. The lift doors opened, I walked uncertainly into the dimly lit cage and, as my stomach rebelled against the upward motion, Mr Chen said, 'You will work for my wife, Lu Si-yan. One day, when you are old enough, you will marry my son. Is that understood?'

Chapter Eleven
When the Roof Fell Down

The rain came first, in torrents. The leaky roof leaked more. We ran out of buckets to place under the ever-increasing number of drips. We used our soup bowls, running to empty them over and over again. We lay in bed at night listening to the tuneful plink, plonk, tink, plop. It was funny at first, until we had to empty bowls throughout the night as well.

The roof caved in one morning, when Mother had gone to the village and Li-hu and I were splashing in puddles in the yard. There was a sickening creak, followed by a loud shudder, which fed into a resounding thud that sent the hens and ducks squawking into the shed. We spun round to find the inside walls of the house exposed – jagged splinters of wood dangling from the tops. A large section of roof was lying across our kitchen table and our bed. A great cloud of dust wheeled in the air before sprinkling down on us.

Li-hu clung to my legs in terror, then, when the dust had settled, he pointed to our house and clapped his hands.

'Look, Si-yan,' he giggled, 'no roof. The roof's all gone.' Then he burst into tears.

I held his hand and stood there anxiously in the pouring rain, wondering what to do. Mother had feared this might happen.

'I don't know what we'll do if the roof falls in, Si-yan,' she had said. 'We don't have the money to get it fixed, and we can't do it ourselves. If only the rain would stop, we could at least patch the worst bits.'

But the rain didn't stop – it pooled its weight and the roof gave up the fight. I walked amongst the debris to find a broken chair, fragments of crockery, toys in pieces. Even the book I was reading had broken its spine. One leg of our bed had cracked in half, but, worst of all, our television, Father's pride and joy, had taken the full force of the collapsing roof and was damaged beyond repair.

Mother arrived back then. We began to clear up the

mess. But we weren't strong enough to remove the larger sheets of wood that straddled the two rooms. I went to the village to fetch help. A team of men left their shops to follow me home, carrying between them a huge red, white and blue striped tarpaulin. In no time, they had removed the remnants of roof and fixed the tarpaulin over the walls. One of them took away the broken chair to mend, while another said he would send his wife with some crockery from his shop. It wouldn't be the best, he said – but we were grateful for anything.

Uncle visited us that evening. There was a smugness about him, tinged with irritation, as he inspected the damage then offered to make arrangements for a replacement roof to be built.

'It is lucky for you that I have a good job and the ability to help,' he said to my mother. 'If my brother had not lived with his head in the clouds, he would have seen to it that you had a proper roof over your heads, and you would not be in the mess you are in now.'

'We are very grateful to you,' replied my mother, head bowed deferentially. 'We will try our best not to become too much of a burden.'

'It would be nothing new,' said Uncle grimly.

When he had gone home, Mother and I sat listening to the rain hammering on the plastic tarpaulin. At length, I asked, 'Why doesn't Uncle like us very much, Mother?'

She sighed and took my hand. 'As you know, Si-yan, your uncle spent many years of his childhood helping to raise your father and being responsible for him. Your father grew up to be a very different sort of person from him, which caused conflict, though your father loved him dearly. Now your uncle finds himself responsible for us, when he has chosen not to have a family of his own and wants to be free of responsibility.'

I thought about this and could see that Uncle might have reason to feel angry, but we had tried so hard to manage on our own since Father died. It wasn't our fault that the roof had caved in. Besides, Uncle had always been welcome in our house. We had shared our meals with him for as long as I could remember. Surely the bond of family was stronger than any selfish considerations.

'But he seems to want us to fail,' I said.

'He doesn't want to believe we might succeed,' corrected my mother. 'And he doesn't want to be proved wrong. Your father proved him wrong by keeping us fed, clothed, housed and happy, despite the fact that he ignored your uncle's advice. He can't conceive of being proved wrong again, especially by a woman and a girl-child.'

I struggled to grasp what Mother was saying. On the one hand, Uncle wanted us to fail, because that was what he expected, and he had to be right. On the other hand, he didn't want us to fail, because he didn't want to be responsible for us.

'Anyway,' sighed my mother, 'he's paying for a new roof, and for that we must be eternally grateful.'

That night, I lay on the broken bed next to my mother and my brother, and determined to work harder still to ensure that we didn't fail.

Halfway through the night, the rain stopped. We woke next morning to a beautiful cloudless sky. Our terraces looked as though they had been sprinkled with diamonds where the sunlight bounced off the drops of rain clinging to our vegetables. Our ducks and hens quacked and squawked relentlessly, stretched and flapped their wings as though celebrating the return of dry weather. Li-hu cavorted among them, hurling feed in the air, trying to catch some before it landed, singing happily.

'I know it's going to be all right,' I said to my mother, as we weeded amongst our crops and checked for marauding insects. 'I know it's going to be all right.'

But it wasn't all right. Several weeks later, we went to market, our rickshaw piled high with vegetables we had been unable to pick during the torrential rain. We hit a deep pothole in the road. It was enough to break the axle, pitching the rickshaw on to its side. Mother and I were thrown on to the road, amidst our valuable produce. When she saw the extent of the damage to the rickshaw, with many of our vegetables smashed and filthy, Mother howled with despair. I put my arms round her, while people gathered to make sure we weren't injured. Mother was in shock, someone thought, but otherwise we were just bruised. They collected together those vegetables which had survived the accident, put them back in our baskets, and a taxi driver offered to take us home.

Travelling in a taxi, the only car I had ever been in, would have been a high point in my life, if I hadn't been so worried about Mother. It was so hot that the driver wound down all the windows, and it was exhilarating to see the world flying by, the wind tugging at my face and hair. Mother sat shaking, gazing straight ahead of her, not saying a word. I held her hand, squeezed it tight again and again, hoping to radiate some of my own will to survive into her being. Only once did she squeeze my hand back, but I took comfort from that and hoped that when we were home she would recover.

When the taxi driver dropped us off, he told me I should put Mother to bed. I did as he advised, and she made no protest. I didn't like to leave her, but I had to collect Li-hu from the village. We returned to find her fast asleep. I was relieved. Li-hu clambered into bed next to her, though it was only early in the afternoon. Soon he was asleep as well.

Our rooms were unbearably hot under the plastic tarpaulin. I wandered outside, swept the yard, tidied the shed, then took a pile of washing down to the river, even though it wasn't washing day. I sat on the river bank, my feet dangling in the cool water, happy to let my cares drift downstream with the current. Things would get better again. We had managed for nearly a year. Mother was suffering from shock, but that would pass. I dipped

Li-hu's trousers in the water and scrubbed them clean. Such tiny trousers for such a bundle of energy.

'Where are you, Si-yan?' I heard him calling.

I turned to see him trundling over the terraces towards me. Then he stopped and laughed.

'Bet you can't catch me,' he screamed.

I jumped to my feet. 'Bet I can,' I yelled.

I gallumphed after him, making dragon noises, captured him and tossed him in the air.

'Mummy's dead,' he said, as I caught him again.

My stomach somersaulted. 'No, Li-hu,' I said. 'Mother's sleeping.'

'Not sleeping,' muttered Li-hu.

I gathered together the washing, took Li-hu's hand and climbed quickly back up to the house. Mother was lying exactly as I had left her. She was so still and quiet that it seemed she had stopped breathing, but I felt her forehead to find she was burning hot, a whisper of air escaping her lips.

'Mother's not dead, Li-hu,' I said with enormous relief. 'Mother's not well, but tomorrow she will be better.'

I prepared our dinner from vegetables that had survived our accident. We waited for Mother to wake up before we ate, because we always sat down together for meals. It grew dark, but still Mother slept. I became more and more anxious, but reasoned that Mother was exhausted from everything she had had to do, that the shock and dismay over the accident had simply been too much for her. A long sleep would do her the world of good.

Uncle arrived then, and for once I was glad to see him, for a grown-up to take over the situation.

'We had an accident, Uncle Ba,' I told him. 'The rickshaw overturned. I think Mother's in shock.'

Uncle went into the other room and came straight back out again.

'Your Mother has a fever. Run to the village and fetch Wen Chunzu,' he ordered. 'He will know what to do.'

I ran as fast as I could, terrified now that every extra second I took would lead to a worsening in my mother's condition. Returning with the village doctor, I was frustrated by the old man's slowness. Much as I urged him on, he complained of his rheumaticky joints and would not be hurried. I took his bag from him in my impatience and supported his elbow as he huffed and puffed his way down the steep pathway to our house.

Uncle welcomed him like a long-lost friend, led him to my mother's side, and shooed me out through the door into the kitchen.

'Bring us cold, damp cloths, and tea for the doctor and myself,' he ordered.

I did as I was told, but was sent away again. Li-hu clung to my legs and cried for his mother. Inside my head, I cried too. I stood up against the door and tried to hear what the doctor was saying. Could I trust this old man with my mother's life?

At last, the door opened and Uncle ushered the doctor out.

'We'll soon see what sort of a fighter she is,' said the doctor gravely. 'The next twenty-four hours will be critical. I'll be back to see her tomorrow morning. In the meantime, keep her cool with cold compresses and moisten her lips regularly. I wish you good day.'

He shook hands with Uncle, who helped him up towards the road, while Li-hu and I slipped through the door to my mother's side. She lay there quietly, an expression of deep peace upon her face, which concealed the battle that raged inside her.

'You can do it, Mother,' I whispered, holding her

hand. 'I know you can do it.'

'You can do it, Mother, I knowed you can do it,' copied Li-hu. 'Wake up soon, Mother.'

Uncle told us that Mother had a very high temperature and fever which it was imperative to bring under control. The doctor had given her medicine to help, but Mother was not strong. She would need constant care for the next few days. He would arrange for someone from the village to sit with Mother that night, and would call in himself first thing in the morning. I was to make up a bed on the kitchen floor and sleep there with Li-hu, so as not to disturb my mother. I wanted so much for him to put his arms round me and tell me that everything was going to be all right. For a brief moment he hesitated in the doorway and I saw the anxiety in his face. I thought he was going to say something more, but then he turned abruptly and headed off home.

I couldn't sleep. The woman from the village, Mrs Jin, arrived, took over from me the mopping of my mother's brow, and left me feeling useless. I wanted her to be there, in case, but I wanted her to sit in a corner and let me care for my mother. Every so often I would get up from my makeshift bed and hover by the door of the bedroom. Sometimes Mother was still and quiet, other times she rolled her head from side to side, moaning and groaning. I didn't know which was worse. At least if she was moving around, even if she was agitated and delirious, I could see that she was alive. When she was motionless, it was hard to tell if she was even breathing. Mrs Jin tried her best to reassure me, but I couldn't help fearing the worst.

In the early hours of the morning, I finally dozed off. I was woken by a horrendous wailing. I rushed to the bedroom door. Mother was tossing around, arms flailing, legs kicking. A sound like an animal in pain came from her lips. Mrs Jin wiped her forehead and spoke gentle words to her. Mother was oblivious. I reached for her hand, squeezed it and caressed it. I kissed her on the cheek and was sure I felt her hand respond to mine.

At last, the wailing stopped, to be replaced by a stillness that mimicked death so perfectly that I thought I had lost her.

'Don't worry, child, she is still fighting,' whispered Mrs Jin. 'Go back to bed now. You will need to be strong to help her.'

I must have fallen into a deep sleep, for when I woke again Uncle had returned and was talking quietly to Mrs Jin.

'Is she all right?' I asked urgently, leaping from my bed.

'She is sleeping peacefully,' said Uncle.

'Oh, thank goodness,' I sobbed, and without even thinking I threw my arms round his waist and held him tight. 'I was so scared she was going to die.'

Uncle stood briefly, awkwardly, and patted my head, before pulling away and addressing Mrs Jin.

'Are you able to stay longer?' he asked. 'Si-yan will make breakfast and I will call by again this evening.'

For the next five days, I looked after Li-hu and helped Mrs Jin to keep my mother comfortable. Gradually, the fever left her. She lay in bed sunken-eyed and exhausted, but peaceful. After ten days, she was able at last to walk around, though not for long, and I was shocked by how thin she had become. She was very quiet, and seemed not to be interested in what was happening on our farm. Uncle had arranged for two men from the village to keep things going, but I knew that we couldn't rely on them for ever, and that we would have to take charge ourselves again soon.

There was to be no relief, however, from the misfortune that dogged us. A drought set in, and the village men returned to their own farms. The temperatures soared to unbearable heights. The earth began to crack in protest, our vegetables wilted. When the well dried up, I brought buckets of water from the river, but I might as well have dropped a teaspoon of water on to a desert.

Only Uncle could provide a lifeline. He sent us boxes of food and called by once a week. He didn't stay to eat with us, and I was glad, for all he did as he wandered over our scorched terraces was to criticise my father for his refusal to take a job at his factory. I wished, how I wished, that we didn't have to be grateful to him, but I began to despair that we would ever be free of the support he provided so unwillingly. Mother seemed unable to rediscover the determination that had kept her going before, and the memory of my father no longer seemed to inspire her. She would stand in the doorway of our house and gaze with utter despair at the wreckage of our crops.

Uncle was sympathetic at first, but he gradually lost

patience at Mother's inability to make any effort to save at least a fraction of our harvest. One evening, he arrived and sent Li-hu and me to fetch fruit from the village. When we came back, we found Mother slumped in a chair, her face harrowed. Uncle had gone. I asked Mother what was the matter. She stared at me, her eyes shot with pain, but she didn't reply, and I was scared, so scared, for all of us.

Chapter Twelve
A Fragile Reed

It was four o'clock, I saw from the clock on the wall as we entered the apartment. Four o'clock in the morning. All was quiet. Mr Chen opened a door into a bedroom.

'This is your room,' he said. 'Get some sleep. You will be woken at eight.'

I nodded and watched the light from the hall squeeze out of the room as he closed the door behind him. Fully clothed, I lay down on the bed, which was more comfortable than any bed I had ever slept on, but, whether from hunger or fear or both, I could not sleep.

Mr Chen's words buffeted my ears relentlessly. '*One day, you will marry my son.*' In my mind I rejected this command over and over again. I was going home. I was going to see my mother again. I wasn't going to stay in this place with people I didn't know. I wasn't going to marry someone I had never even met. How could my uncle do this to me, how could he?

I must have dozed eventually, because I was woken by a sense that there was somebody in my room. In a spill of light from the hall, I saw a silhouetted figure hovering in the doorway. Then I heard Mr Chen's sharp voice saying, 'Come away, Yimou,' followed by the shutting of the door. Was it the boy I was supposed to marry who had stood there? I leapt out of bed, desperate to lock myself in, but there was no key. I got back into bed, pulled the blanket right up to my chin, and lay there listening to every sound, eyes fixed on the door, heart thumping wildly.

At home I had shared a bed with my mother and Li-hu, so it was strange all of a sudden to have a bed to myself, a bed with a proper mattress and pillow. As the room grew brighter I looked around. The walls were painted white, the curtains were decorated with white cranes flying across a pale blue background, the same colour as the blanket, there was a small wooden table with a lamp on it, a sink in the corner with a mirror above, a low chest of drawers, a wooden chair, and on the floor was a beautiful silk rug.

'This is your room,' Mr Chen had said. It was a pretty room, a clean room, a finer room than any I had seen before. 'This is my room,' I tried out, rejecting the idea even as I said it.

I was beginning to swelter under the weight of the blanket, and curiosity was getting the better of my fear of intruders. With one swift movement, I thrust the blanket aside, leapt across the room and peered out through the curtains.

We were miles up in the air! I'd had no idea. A dull mist clung to the dozens of bright white apartment blocks on either side, and hovered eerily below. It was thin enough though for me to be able to make out the decrepit tops of older apartment blocks on slopes further down. Around and beyond them lay a vast, desolate, rubble wasteland. Where was this place? I wondered. Not a hint of colour punctured the loud whiteness of the new apartment buildings, the mottled white of the mist and the blotchy greyness of the older landscape. I felt as though I were looking out on a ghost city where some unimaginable catastrophe had occurred.

A loud knock brought me to attention.

'It is eight o'clock, Lu Si-yan,' called a woman's voice. 'Come and have your breakfast.'

However much I was anxious about what I would find outside my room and beyond, I was hungry enough to allow my stomach to lead. I opened the door slowly and peered into the hall, which disappeared round a corner in one direction. It was deserted, but a delicious assortment of smells wafted by, and noises were coming from the other direction, not too far away from my room. I walked cautiously towards them, skirting round two other doorways in case they opened. When I reached the end of the hall, I hesitated outside a half-open door, waited for a loud banging to stop, then knocked gently.

'Come in, child,' said the woman's voice.

I stepped nervously into a brightly lit kitchen. It was full of the sort of equipment I had only ever seen before in shop windows. On a table in the middle of the room, a porcelain bowl and soup spoon and a pair of chopsticks were waiting expectantly. Mrs Chen, for I assumed that was who she was, appeared from behind a cupboard door.

My jaw dropped with astonishment when I saw her. She was extraordinarily beautiful, immaculately dressed in the finest silk and pearls. She seemed to have stepped straight out of the pages of a magazine.

She looked me up and down, her steady gaze making me feel thoroughly shabby. But she suddenly smiled and said, 'You are like a fragile reed. One puff of wind and you will break in two. We need to feed you up, Lu Si-yan. Sit down and eat.'

She gave me a hot, moist towel with which to wipe my hands and face, then brought a bowl of soup followed by dishes of chicken, vegetables and rice. So much food, and all for me, since it seemed that I was to eat alone.

While I filled my bowl with soup, Mrs Chen sat down in silence at the other side of the table. I began to eat, but became aware that she was watching my every move, which made me feel awkward and clumsy. Though I tried to remember everything I had been told about good table manners, I failed to stop a dribble of soup stealing down my chin. I wiped it as furtively as I could on the back of my hand, only to glance up and see that Mrs Chen's lips had pursed briefly with disapproval before settling again into their charitable smile. When I helped myself to rice, a cluster of grains fell on to the table. The lips pursed again. I wished she would say something, anything, rather than just sit there watching.

All pleasure in the meal evaporated under Mrs Chen's critical eye. I had never eaten better, but I had never enjoyed a meal less. I ate as much as I was able, not daring to leave too much in case it was taken as an insult, then smiled timidly and said, 'Thank you, Mrs Chen. That was delicious.'

'We'll soon tidy up your manners,' Mrs Chen replied, smiling back. 'Now, when you've finished washing up, I'll take you to have your hair cut and buy you some new clothes.'

With that, she sailed out of the kitchen, leaving me to discover for myself the sink piled high with dirty pans and dishes.

I wasn't used to a tap that delivered hot water, so immediately scalded myself, nor had I come across something called 'washing-up liquid', which I found by the sink. I read the label and, as directed, squirted some into the running water, then I gave a few extra squirts in case I hadn't put in enough. I watched with amusement as the bubbles appeared, then horror as they frothed over the side of the sink on to the floor. I grabbed a cloth and tried to wipe up the mess, but water began to overflow as well because I had forgotten to turn off the tap. Some of the pans were very sticky. I scrubbed them hard, then left them to drain while I attacked the dishes which, when clean, I balanced on top of the pans. One of them slid to the floor with a resounding crash, which summoned Mrs Chen.

She found me rooted panic-stricken to the spot, surrounded by hundreds of pieces of broken porcelain and rivulets of water. She looked at me, at the porcelain scattered all over the floor, and beyond me to the pile of dishes and pans. She picked up a pan, inspected it, put it down, picked up the cloth which I had used to wipe the floor, inspected it, put it down.

'The cloth is for drying dishes,' she said.

'I'm sorry,' I muttered.

'There is a broom in the cupboard. Be sure you sweep up every last splinter. We wouldn't want to cut ourselves, would we?'

'No, Mrs Chen,' I mumbled.

'The pans will need washing again,' she continued. 'It's early days. I'm sure you will do better next time.'

'Yes, Mrs Chen.'

I swept and swept the floor, every last millimetre of it, until I was sure Mrs Chen could not possibly detect even the smallest fragment of porcelain. Then I scoured and scraped and scrubbed the pans, before drying them carefully on a clean cloth. When Mrs Chen reappeared, she didn't look at the floor or the pans, simply glanced at the table, pointed out a grain of rice, and asked me to wipe it up before we went out.

As I stood beside her in the lift, smothered by the strength of her perfume, I felt thoroughly confused. I was in the most beautiful apartment, with a room of my own, eating the most delicious food I had ever tasted, going out to buy the first new clothes I had had in years. Things could have been a million times worse, yet I was full of foreboding. It seemed I was there to do exactly as Mrs Chen wished, to be shaped and moulded in whatever way she saw fit. I didn't want to have my hair cut. Why should I have my hair cut just because Mrs Chen said I had to? But I didn't dare defy her. Her smile was barbed. It failed to touch her eyes, where I sensed pitilessness lurking not far below the surface.

Chapter Thirteen
Things Must Improve

We drove into town. Mrs Chen had her own car! Even Uncle didn't have a car. The lift took us right down underneath the apartment block into a huge parking area, where Mrs Chen opened the doors to a big silver saloon and told me to get in the back. As we drove out into the street, I was astonished to see how many cars there were driving up and down – not just taxis, but cars with ordinary people in them. We travelled along a wide road where apartment blocks towered above us, all of them new, and brilliantly lit, glossy-fronted shops were filled with slender mannequins sporting the most extravagant fashions. Did people really wear such clothes? I wondered.

I became aware that Mrs Chen was observing me again, glancing in her mirror. The smile appeared when she saw that I had noticed her.

'Try not to gawp, Lu Si-yan, it's not very becoming. We don't want you to look like an ignorant peasant girl, do we?'

She drew up outside a row of smaller shops, the second of which advertised itself as a hairdressers and beauty salon. The owner came to the shop door the minute she saw Mrs Chen, held it open for her and greeted her respectfully.

'The child needs her hair tamed, cut in a short bob, I think, with a straight fringe out of her eyes. You will also need to work on her hands. They're ingrained with dirt. Heaven knows what she's been using them for.'

'Yes, Mrs Chen. Certainly, Mrs Chen.'

Mrs Chen gave her orders and sat down with a magazine, while an assistant brought her tea. I watched tearfully in the mirror, my thick black hair falling to the ground in large clumps, a neat, well-behaved bob appearing in its place. My hands were scoured and oiled, my nails carefully clipped into immaculate crescent moons. The manager sought Mrs Chen's approval, who declared the result a great improvement, and I was whisked off for the next stage in my transformation.

I was quite excited by the prospect of new clothes – clothes that fitted, beautiful clothes like those I could see on some of the girls who passed us, girls I couldn't help turning to admire, even though I could see Mrs Chen's lips tightening. Perhaps I might look as pretty as they did.

We stopped at a small clothes shop. Once again the manager rushed to open the door for us and to serve Mrs Chen.

'I want something in the way of a uniform for this child,' she said. 'You know the sort of thing. A servant's uniform, calf-length, perhaps in black or navy with a white collar.'

'Certainly, Madam. What about this?'

The manager pulled from a rail a plain navy dress, very straight, a small pleat at the back of the skirt, long-sleeved, buttoned at the wrists, with a white collar.

'Try it on, Lu Si-yan.'

When I emerged from the changing room, Mrs Chen clapped her hands.

'Perfect,' she smiled. 'We'll have two, plus two plain white blouses, one of those navy coats over there, plus two pairs of socks, underwear and pyjamas – nothing too fancy.'

Purchases in hand, I was then taken to a shoe shop, where Mrs Chen chose a pair of heavy black lace-ups.

'Good and sturdy,' she said. 'Nothing frivolous. We wouldn't want to damage your young feet, would we?'

On the way back to the car, she told me what a lucky girl I was to have so much money spent on me, and that as soon as we were home I was to change into my new clothes and throw my old ones away.

It was nearly midday by the time we returned to the apartment. I had five minutes in which to change, then I was to go to the study to receive instructions about my duties. I stared in the mirror and didn't recognise the person standing there. She looked older, thinner, more serious than the girl I remembered. There was a shadowy air of resignation about her as well, which I instantly fought by hiding my favourite old blouse behind the chest-of-drawers. Mrs Chen wasn't going to have all of me.

I left my room reluctantly and went in search of the study. Passing one of the doors in the hall, I was sure I heard voices. I stopped to listen. All was silent. Should I go in? There was the sound of a pan clattering in the kitchen. I continued in that direction, heard a door open behind me, and turned to see Mrs Chen emerging from the room I had just hesitated by.

'Where are you going, child?' she said irritably. 'Can't you obey a simple instruction? I said the study.'

'I don't know which is the study.'

The smile appeared. 'Of course, how silly of me. It's this room here.'

She showed me in and sat me down on a wooden chair facing a wall covered with shelf upon shelf of pristine-spined books, while she stood at the window, her back to me.

'You will rise at six o'clock,' she said. 'Lateness will not be tolerated. Cook will leave you a list in the kitchen of foodstuffs to prepare for breakfast. You will do as he asks, then you will lay the table in the dining room. Four settings. You will eat alone in the kitchen when we have finished. You will find everything you need in the large cupboard. At six forty-five promptly you will return to your room to clean yourself up and make your bed. I will not expect to see you again until you come for your breakfast at seven-thirty. After you have eaten, you will clear up, having learned from your errors this morning.'

She smiled, before continuing with a list that included washing, ironing, cleaning, as well as preparing and clearing up after meals. I struggled hard to take it all in. It seemed I wasn't to be free each day until eight o'clock in the evening, when I was to retire to my room.

'Can you sew?' asked Mrs Chen.

I nodded. I had often sewn patches in Li-hu's trousers and darned my own clothes.

'Good. After lunch you can make a start by replacing the buttons on these shirts, but first I shall introduce you to Cook and you can help to prepare our lunch.'

I followed her out of the study and along to the kitchen. There, to my astonishment, she took hold of the arm of the young man standing by the stove and swung him round to face me. Her whole manner was suddenly smiling and flirtatious.

'Xiong Fei, this is Lu Si-yan, who has come to help you in the kitchen, haven't you, Lu Si-yan? Show her how we do things here, won't you, Xiong Fei? I'd be so grateful to you.'

She patted him possessively on the shoulder. Xiong Fei smiled.

'Yes, Mrs Chen. Of course, Mrs Chen.'

'I'll leave you to it, then. Call me if there are any problems.'

She patted him again on the shoulder, then sailed gracefully past me out of the room, leaving a trail of her perfume to mingle familiarly with the aromas from Xiong Fei's cooking.

I stood there uncertainly, waiting for him to speak first, when I thought I heard him mutter 'witch' under his breath. He looked at me steadily, winked and said, 'Don't look so terrified, Lu Si-yan. I won't bite.' Then he whispered, 'I leave that to other people. Now be careful what you say in here – the walls have ears.'

Unwittingly I glanced round at the walls, causing Xiong Fei to smile, a big wide smile which lit up his eyes. He wasn't particularly good-looking, but his face was strong and full of mischief. I blushed shyly.

'You're so young,' he said. 'Why aren't you at home with your parents?' And then, suddenly businesslike: 'Prepare these vegetables for me, would you, Lu Si-yan.'

A shadow passed by the door, then we heard another door closing.

'Be careful not to chop your fingers off, Lu Si-yan,' Xiong Fei smiled. 'The knives are very sharp, and the sight of blood makes me faint clean away.'

I smiled back. I began chopping and shaping the vegetables, slowly at first because I didn't want to make any mistakes, then more confidently when Xiong Fei started to whistle while he worked.

'I bet you can't chop onions without crying, Lu Si-yan,' he said. 'They make me cry so much I could flood the Yangtse with my tears.'

I giggled self-consciously. 'I'll try,' I said.

He passed the onions to me.

'No tears, then,' he said. 'I shall be watching.'

I cut the top off a first onion, peeled back the brown skin, then sliced down to the root. As I chopped it all into small pieces, tears welled up in my eyes and one escaped down my cheek.

'Oh, my poor Lu Si-yan,' wailed Xiong Fei dramatically. 'Please don't cry. You will make my heart break. You failed the test, by the way. I will do the onions. You do the ginger.'

I had more fun preparing that meal than I had had for a very long time, though we were careful not to attract Mrs Chen's attention. Xiong Fei told me that he was an art student. He cooked for the Chens to pay his college fees, and had been with them for six months. He arrived, cooked, then left, three times a day, seven days a week.

'Have you met their son?' I couldn't help asking.

'Never. I've only met Mr Chen once, and that was when I applied for the job. Mornings and evenings I cook for five people, including the domestic, but I go before anyone sits down to eat. Lunchtimes I cook for two or three. If nothing else, little silk swallow, you will eat well while I am here.'

'Have there been other servants?'

'You have replaced an old housekeeper, Mrs Wu, who had been with the Chens for eighteen years. Two weeks ago, Mrs Chen told Mrs Wu, without any warning, that her services were no longer required.'

That made me feel terrible. 'Do you know why she was sent away?' I asked.

Before he could answer, Mrs Chen strode into the kitchen, looked challengingly at Xiong Fei, and asked me why the table hadn't been set.

'You are rather slow today, Xiong Fei,' she said. 'I hope you are not being distracted from your work.'

'Not at all, Mrs Chen. Lu Si-yan and I are getting along very well,' he replied, fixing her directly with his eyes.

Mrs Chen was clearly unsure how to take this but, after a moment's hesitation, she smiled sweetly and said, 'Good, I'm glad to hear it.'

She moved next to him, took him by the elbow, and continued, 'I would like to make it quite clear, though, that I will not tolerate gossip. Is that understood?'

'Yes, Mrs Chen.' Xiong Fei and I both nodded.

'Then I shall expect lunch to be ready in fifteen minutes' time.'

As soon as she had left the room, Xiong Fei picked up a knife and made stabbing noises towards the door.

'Grrrrr, I hate her,' he growled through gritted teeth. 'Pawing me like a pet dog. If I didn't need the money so much, I would tell her what I thought of her and her miserable job.'

He turned back to his cooking, muttering angrily to himself. I went into the dining room to set the table. How many for, I wondered – two or three? If it was three, who else was coming? Was I supposed to lay a place for myself, even though I would not be eating with them? Perhaps I should lay only one place, for Mrs Chen herself. I returned to the kitchen, where Xiong Fei was putting on his coat, ready to leave.

'I don't know how many place settings to lay,' I said, wishing so hard that he could stay.

'Always two unless Mrs Chen is lunching out.'

'But I'm to eat separately, she told me.'

'The other place is for her mother-in-law. She lives here too.'

'I haven't met her,' I said.

'She's a lovely old lady,' said Xiong Fei. 'Not at all like Mrs Chen. See you this evening, Lu Si-yan. Good luck.'

I went back into the dining room and laid the table for two people. What should I do next, though? I wondered. Was I supposed to bring in the food? Should I wait to make sure that everything was all right?

Too late. There were voices outside. The door opened and a tiny, frail old lady in a wheelchair entered the room. Behind her was Mrs Chen.

'What are you doing here?' she snapped. 'I thought I told you that you were to eat separately.'

'I didn't know if you wanted me to bring the food through.'

'That should have been done already. I see I shall have to do it myself.'

'Who is this pretty young child?' interrupted the old

lady, in a voice as smooth as silk. 'Won't you introduce me, Shumei?'

The lips pursed, the eyes tightened. I could see that Mrs Chen was livid, though she tried to hide it.

'Just our new domestic, Mother. She has a lot to learn, I am afraid.'

'Ah, to replace dear old Mrs Wu. So sad that she decided to leave us after so many years. Tell me, child, what is your name?'

Mrs Chen jumped in before I could reply. 'Her name is Lu Si-yan. Now, Mother, if you don't mind, she has work to do.'

'Can you read, Lu Si-yan?' the old lady persisted.

Again, Mrs Chen replied for me. 'She's a peasant girl. Of course she can't read. Why would she need to?'

'I can read, Mrs Chen,' I couldn't help saying. 'I learnt at school.'

Mrs Chen turned on me. 'How dare you contradict me!' she spat. 'Who do you think you are?'

'I'm sorry, Mrs Chen, I just –'

'I should like Lu Si-yan to read to me.'

This was made as a statement by the old lady, not a request. Mrs Chen looked as though she couldn't believe what she was hearing. She took a deep breath, grabbed hold of the handles of her mother-in-law's wheelchair and pushed her roughly to her place at the table. 'Impossible,' she declared. 'Her day is full already. And now, if you don't mind, I insist that she return to her work, while we sit down to eat before our meal is cold. Lu Si-yan, you may clear the table in half an hour. In the meantime, there is plenty of washing-up for you to make a start on.'

She smiled sweetly at both of us, then hustled me out of the room before her mother-in-law could respond.

Alone in the kitchen, I tried not to repeat my errors of the morning. I was exhausted. My head was pounding. All I wanted was to go home, for this nightmare to end. I finished cleaning a saucepan, sat down at the table, and put my head in my hands. *This* was to be my home. *These* people were my family. I rebelled against every notion of it. I wanted my mother. She would never willingly have let this happen.

I must have fallen asleep, for the next thing I knew, Mrs Chen was slamming dishes down by the sink.

'Half an hour I said, Lu Si-yan. Half an hour, then clear the table. That was forty-five minutes ago. Your lunch is cold, you will have to go without. When you have finished washing these dishes, you will find the sewing waiting for you in the study.' She smiled then. 'I'm sure things must improve.'

'Please, Mrs Chen, please can I send a letter to my mother and tell her where I am?' I begged.

'I don't think that's a good idea, Lu Si-yan,' she replied. 'Your mother doesn't want you. That's why you're here.'

I didn't stop for a moment for the rest of that first day. When Xiong Fei arrived early that evening, he found me polishing silverware at the kitchen table. I was so relieved to see him that, to my embarrassment, I burst into tears. He closed the door and leant against it so that no one could come in, then called me over to him. I pressed my head against his chest and sobbed.

'What's the matter, little sparrow?' he asked, stroking my hair.

'Swallow, not sparrow,' I spluttered through my sobs.

'You look like a drab little sparrow at the moment, rather than a sleek and shiny swallow. Has the wicked witch been nasty to you?'

'She won't let me write a letter to my mother.'

'Then write it and I shall send it for you,' said Xiong Fei.

'But you'll get into trouble.'

'Only if I'm caught.'

A movement of the door handle made him grab my arm and pull me across the kitchen to the sink, where he turned on the tap and began to splash my face with water.

'What were you – what on earth are you doing?'

I swivelled my head to catch Mrs Chen staring at us in absolute astonishment.

'Lu Si-yan rubbed her eyes and got silver polish in them. I'm just trying to wash it out.'

'Are you indeed? How very kind of you, Xiong Fei.' The voice purred but the lips were pursed. 'Now perhaps you'd like to prepare our meal, which is what we pay you for.'

'Yes, Mrs Chen.'

'As for you, Lu Si-yan – be a little more careful, will you, so as not to disrupt the rest of the staff?'

'Yes, Mrs Chen,' I replied, water running down my face from my sodden hair.

As soon as she was out of earshot, Xiong Fei shook

with stifled laughter.

'Did you see her face, Lu Si-yan?' Then, more serious, he said, 'Don't ever let her see you cry, little sparrow, for she'll know she's broken you then. Cry on my shoulder or alone in your room, but never in front of her.'

I nodded and thanked him for his kindness.

We worked in silence for a time. I could hear men's voices drifting along the hall from distant rooms. Was I about to meet the boy I had been told I was to marry? Yimou? I wanted to ask Xiong Fei to take me away with him when he left so that I would never have to meet this Yimou. I crept into the dining room to set the table, then crept out again as quickly as I could, back to the safety of the kitchen.

'Tell me to mind my own business if you like,' said Xiong Fei, looking at me quizzically, 'but how old are you?'

'Eleven,' I replied quietly.

'And are they paying you to work here?'

I glanced towards the door, praying that Mrs Chen wasn't listening in on us, for I was sure that this constituted more than just gossip, and that we would suffer

86

the consequences. I bit my lip and shook my head. How could I explain that Mr Chen owned me, that he had bought me from my uncle, that I was his to do what he liked with, that this was my family now?

'It's disgraceful,' exploded Xiong Fei. 'If they don't pay you, they're treating you like a slave. I shall tell them so. I shall put a stop to it.'

I shook my head vehemently. 'No, Xiong Fei, no. There's nothing you can do. It's not like that.'

In my heart I felt it was worse than that. Far worse to be bought, shaped and moulded as the perfect obedient future daughter-in-law, than simply to work for no pay. Was that what Mrs Chen was doing?

'Then what is it like?' asked Xiong Fei gently. 'Why aren't you at home with your mother?'

'She didn't want me to go, I know she didn't want me to go, but she couldn't afford to keep me, not on her own, not once Li-hu was born and Father died and she was ill and there was the drought. Uncle said it was the only way for Mother and Li-hu to survive.'

I could feel myself becoming tearful again. Don't let Mrs Chen see you cry, I said to myself.

'Mr Chen bought me from my uncle. When I'm old

enough, I'm to marry their son. It's been agreed.'

Xiong Fei stared at me in total disbelief. 'But you're just a baby,' he said. Then, as we heard footsteps, 'Write that letter, Lu Si-yan. I'll post it to your mother if it's the last thing I do.'

Chapter Fourteen
A River of Hope

I didn't meet Yimou that evening, nor at any time during my first few days. I heard him sometimes – I think it was him – laughing rather too loudly, breaking something precious judging by Mrs Chen's screams, knocking on my bedroom door then disappearing at the chilling sound of his father's voice. I tried to conjure up a picture of him, but it was never flattering. I didn't want him to be attractive, didn't want him to be kind and caring – that way it would be easy to hate him. I wanted to go home. I would rather have remained unmarried for the whole of my life and be with my mother, than become the daughter-in-law of Mrs Chen.

My room became my sanctuary. I dreaded leaving it in the morning, couldn't wait to rediscover it in the evening. I spent hours standing by the window, watching the mist and smog spiralling lazily round the grey tenement blocks lower down, hoping for a gap to appear so that I could see beyond.

Then, suddenly, after nine days, it cleared. Watery yellow sunlight seeped through the thinness of my curtains, rousing me before my wake-up bell. I leapt from my bed to gaze out on a brilliant blue sky. I was amazed to discover that, far below, beyond the graveyard of fallen dwellings, a river, much much bigger than the one at home, was leading its own life. Boats of all shapes and sizes were travelling up and down, ant-sized people were busying themselves on the shores, an endless stream of vehicles was carrying produce to and from the boats.

In some curious way, that river spelled freedom. It came from somewhere and it went somewhere. It was my river of hope. As long as I could see it, the door of my prison would stay open.

I was delighted to learn that Mrs Chen was going out that afternoon. She gave me an impossibly long list of duties, and locked the door behind her, but she couldn't dampen my spirits. The moment she left I set about my work with renewed vigour. Even the thought of the criticism I would undoubedly suffer later couldn't spoil my mood. I sang as I worked, all the songs I used to sing with my father. I danced around with a damp cloth, stood on the broom and seesawed backwards and forwards, polished the top of the sideboard with a flourish of the duster.

A slight movement by the door caught my eye. I stopped, rigid with fright.

'It's good to see you enjoying your work, Lu Si-yan.'

The voice as smooth as silk. Mrs Hong, in her wheelchair, eyes sparkling with amusement.

'I'm sorry, Mrs Hong. I hope I didn't disturb you.'

'Apology not accepted,' said Mrs Hong. 'There's not enough singing in this household. Now, dear, what about making us a nice pot of tea, and then you can read to me.'

'But what about the dusting, Mrs Hong? Mrs Chen said –'

'I shall tell my daughter-in-law that the dust would wait but I wouldn't. I shall be in my room, whirling around like an impatient child, so be quick with our tea so that I don't exhaust myself.'

She grinned at me mischievously before she spun

away down the hall, leaving me holding the duster and wondering whether it would be all right to do as she asked. I decided that I couldn't refuse her and would just have to hope that Mrs Chen would not be angry with me. Besides, I was curious to explore the other wing of the apartment, to discover where Mrs Hong spent her time.

I walked carefully along the pale, intricately patterned silk carpet, carrying a tray with the pot of boiling hot tea and two delicate porcelain bowls, scared stiff that I might spill some. Mrs Hong heard the bowls rattle and opened her door wide.

'Bless you, child. Come in and put the tray on the table, then sit yourself down while I pour. I'm not totally useless, you'll see.'

'Of course not,' I said, feeling very awkward and shy. 'I'm sure you can do lots of things.'

'If I'm allowed to,' grimaced Mrs Hong. 'Everyone fusses so. My legs gave up years ago, and my eyesight's not so good – which is why I would like you to read to me – but the rest of me is in full working order.'

As if to prove her point, she picked up the teapot with a flourish, began pouring, then raised it to a great height above each bowl and lowered it again while pouring all the time. She didn't spill a drop and looked thoroughly pleased with herself.

'I'll teach you how to do it one day,' she said. 'Now, drink up, then tell me a little about yourself. My son says that you are an orphan, poor child, and that your uncle has asked us to train you in domestic service until you are old enough to seek work for yourself. It was lucky for you that we had a vacancy. So strange that Mrs Wu left so suddenly.'

I was dumbfounded. Not only had Mr Chen kept the truth about Mrs Wu's departure from his mother, but he had lied to her about me. I wasn't an orphan. How dare he say that my mother was dead? She wasn't dead. I was going to go home to her. She wasn't dead.

'You are very pale, Lu Si-yan,' Mrs Hong said quietly, 'and so very young. I hope you will turn to me for help if you have any worries.'

That silky voice wrapped itself comfortingly, coaxingly round me. I looked up at her kindly face and wanted to share everything with her there and then, but how could I, without revealing that her son and daughter-in-law had lied to her.

I nodded my head and said simply, 'I shall enjoy reading to you, Mrs Hong. I used to read to my father.'

'Then after we have finished our tea you shall choose a book and we shall begin.'

I asked Mrs Hong about the river down below. When she told me it was the Yangtse, I realised just how far from home I had travelled.

'What are all the fallen buildings?'

'That's the old town,' Mrs Hong explained. 'It is being pulled down because it is liable to flood when the level of the river rises. This new town was built and everyone was rehoused here. Those who farmed the land further down have been given jobs in factories.'

'My father was a farmer,' I said. 'He would have hated to work in a factory.'

'So should I, my dear, so should I. But the youngsters, well, many of them prefer it. It can be easy money compared to toiling on the land.'

'I like to be out in the fresh air,' I said, and wondered when I might be allowed to go outside and explore.

The books in Mrs Hong's room, unlike those in the study, were dog-eared and inviting. I chose one at random, sought Mrs Hong's approval, then sat down to read. I was nervous at first, certain I would not be up to the task, but as the story unfolded and Mrs Hong nodded encouragement, closing her eyes to listen more attentively, I relaxed and began to lose myself in the story. Page after page went by, my voice the only sound to break the peace.

A clock struck suddenly. Mrs Hong opened her eyes.

'You read very well, Lu Si-yan. Mrs Wu was a trifle monotonous, bless her. We will do this again, but now I am going to help you with your dusting.'

I was amazed that Mrs Hong would even consider helping me. She had reached her door before I could attempt to stop her, and began hurtling down the hall as though in a race. Just as she reached the door to the apartment, it opened and she crashed into it, causing it to rebound into the shopping-laden Mrs Chen. I was so shocked, and at the same time the scene struck me as so comical, that I hooted with laughter. A brief, hysterical hoot, but it was noted even in the confusion. For a moment Mrs Chen stood thunderstruck. Then she dropped her shopping, pushed past Mrs Hong and made a grab for me.

'How dare you mock me!' she shrieked. 'Who gave

you permission to enter this area of our apartment the minute my back was turned?'

'You know very well it was me,' said Mrs Hong calmly. 'I am to blame, so please don't take it out on the poor child.'

'"The poor child" has been nothing but trouble since she arrived. She needs to understand her place here, while you, dear mother-in-law, need to understand that old women do not go racing around in wheelchairs with the servants.'

'You, dear daughter-in-law, need to understand *your* place here. I am the head of this household and if I wish Lu Si-yan to read to me then so she shall.'

'We'll see about that,' fumed Mrs Chen. 'Go to the kitchen now, Lu Si-yan. I shall expect to find that you have done everything I asked.'

She took hold of the arms of the wheelchair, turned it round and pushed Mrs Hong back to her room.

Chapter Fifteen
A Prisoner

A month went by, a month in which I began to feel like a prisoner. Apart from the shopping trip on my first morning, I hadn't left the apartment. Mrs Chen filled every minute of my day with chores, appearing from nowhere time and again to check that I was doing as she had asked and doing it properly. Her criticisms were endless and soul-destroying.

My only lifeline was Xiong Fei. His arrival three times a day lifted my despair. Mrs Chen clearly suspected as much, and kept a careful eye on us, flirting more and more outrageously with him, while doing her best to make me look like a foolish little girl. We laughed in turn at her arrogance and stupidity, laughter which kept me going from one mealtime to the next.

During that long first month, I saw neither Mr Chen

nor Yimou. They left the apartment immediately after breakfast, and disappeared when they returned in the evenings into the rooms that were out of bounds to me. I felt that perhaps Yimou was being kept away from me deliberately. And then, on the fifth Saturday after Uncle had taken me to market, Mrs Chen informed me that from the next day, and every Sunday onwards, I was to cook for the whole family, all three meals, and serve them as well.

'Your uncle assured Mr Chen that you can cook, so now you can prove it,' she said, smiling, as though setting a test in which she was sure I would fail.

She gave me strict instructions on every aspect of what I was to cook that first Sunday, when it was to be served, how it was to be served and what was expected of me. I was aghast. How could I possibly do it all on my own? My mind froze as she spoke, unable to take in the bombardment of minute details. And then, worse – as she left the room, I realised that I was bound to meet Yimou for the first time.

Xiong Fei's arrival that Saturday evening did little to cheer me up. He talked me step by step through the preparation of the dishes I was to cook, muttering angrily about Mrs Chen's spitefulness in setting me such a task. He was also furious about the fact that, without any warning or discussion, he was to lose a whole day's work.

'She just uses people, then spits them out when she no longer has any need for them. Now she asks you, an eleven-year-old, to do the work of an experienced chef. She's using you like a slave, Lu Si-yan. Have you written to your mother yet?'

I shook my head miserably. 'I can't tell her, I just can't. She can't take me back, Uncle made that clear. How can I worry her when there's nothing she can do to help?'

'Then give me your uncle's address and let me write to him. He's your family. He should be looking after you.'

'Uncle hates me. It was his idea to send me away in the first place.'

'But how can you stay here, Lu Si-yan?'

'I have no choice,' I replied.

I have no choice, I said to myself over and over again in my room later that evening, as I gazed out of the window only to discover that the river had disappeared once more beneath a thick blanket of mist. I had thought about escaping, just simply running away, but I had no money, Mrs Chen was careful to keep the apartment door locked, and where would I go, anyway? My future looked as bleak as the shadowland below, my determination to go home to my mother faltering when little more than a month had passed.

Chapter Sixteen
Have to Kiss it Better

Sunday arrived with the wake-up bell at five-thirty. Though the sun had yet to rise, I could see that the mist and smog were lying in wait for me, blotting out the river and its hint of hope. I dragged myself into my uniform, exhausted before a day that promised me no rest had even begun. I looked in the mirror and wondered anew at who the girl standing there was. The air of resignation had now overwhelmed her. You're here to stay, the girl in the mirror seemed to say. There's no point in fighting it.

I was grateful to discover that Xiong Fei had chopped up some of the vegetables in advance and left them in the refrigerator, as well as preparing the plates of preserved meats and pickles. I struggled to remember what he had said about oven temperatures, how much oil to use, which spices belonged with which dish. I set the table in the dining room while trying to sort things out in my mind, then returned to the kitchen to measure out noodles and rice and carve up the chicken and beef. How well these people eat, I reflected, compared to my family and friends back home. But how well are they going to eat today? I couldn't help smiling wryly. I flattened a chicken breast, picked up a cleaver, and sliced through the top of my finger.

Droplets of blood fell to the floor as I dashed for the cold tap. I held my finger under the running water, desperate to curb the spill of red but, though it wasn't too serious a cut, the blood kept flowing. I grabbed the teacloth and wrapped it round my hand. A deep red stain spread relentlessly through the material as I ransacked the drawers for something to bind the cut. All I could think of was that time was passing and I hadn't even started cooking. I found some plastic film, tore off a strip and wound it round and round the top of my finger, hoping to contain the bleeding for long enough to enable me to cook and serve the meal.

I could hear voices. My time was nearly up. I plunged the rice into a pan of boiling water, heated the oil in two woks, tipped in some chopped onion, garlic and ginger, finished carving the chicken and beef, separated them into the two woks, tossed them about in the oil, added various sauces, herbs and spices, and prayed that I had got it right. I carried the cold dishes through to the dining room, placed them round the edges of the revolving tray in the middle of the table, and returned to the kitchen to find Mrs Chen standing there.

'There is blood on the floor, Lu Si-yan.' She pointed to the teacloth. 'There is blood on this teacloth, Lu Si-yan. Do you have any idea how unhygienic that is? Do you have any idea what a health risk that is?'

'I'm sorry, Mrs Chen. I cut my finger and –'

'I don't care if you cut your throat. I will not have my kitchen contaminated by you. How do I know that you haven't infected our food with your blood?'

'I was very careful to –'

'Careful you are not, Lu Si-yan. Careful people do not drop plates, do not spill food, do not take slices out of their fingers. You will throw this teacloth away, you will clean up your blood with disinfectant, and I shall expect you to serve us in ten minutes.'

Behind her, the saucepan of rice bubbled angrily, came to the boil, and hissing water spilled all over the top of the oven. Mrs Chen turned to look, then stormed out of the room, leaving me to fume at the injustice of her attack. I hurled the soiled cloth into the bin. I mopped savagely at the blood-spotted floor. I felt like screaming obscenities for the whole world to hear. I was doing my best. Why was my best never good enough?

I stamped over to the oven and was sickened to find that one of the sauces over the meat had reduced to almost nothing, while the other was thick and glutinous. The meat itself was sticking to the bottoms of the woks. I poured some boiling water from the rice into the woks and stirred frenziedly, trying at the same time to free the meat and thin the sauces, some of which spattered down the front of my uniform. The clock on the wall told me I had two minutes left before I had to present myself in the dining room. I drained the rice and tipped it into a bowl.

I stood outside the dining room with the bowl of rice. This was the moment I had been dreading.

I saw Mrs Hong first, who smiled kindly. Seated next

to her, Mr Chen simply nodded. By his side, the finely dressed young man stared at me and his cheeks flushed pink. He was so handsome that I must have gawped, because Mrs Chen said sharply, 'Don't play the peasant, please, Lu Si-yan.'

I placed the bowl in the centre of the table, stood back and waited for instructions. There was silence, then Mrs Chen said, 'Where are the hot towels, Lu Si-yan?'

My stomach plunged. Nobody had said anything about providing hot towels at breakfast time. It was first thing in the morning. Surely hot towels weren't needed when everyone had so recently washed.

'I'm sorry, Mrs Chen, I didn't realise –'

'We always have hot towels, before every meal. I'm sure I told you. Too late now. We'll have to do without.'

'No hot towels, Grandma.' Yimou leant conspiratorially across the table to whisper loudly to Mrs Hong.

'No, dear, not today. Never mind, though. It won't harm us.'

'What are you waiting for now, Lu Si-yan? Dish out some rice and hand round the cold meats.'

Mrs Chen tried to make herself appear agreeable, a smile on her lips after she spoke, while her husband sat

105

patiently waiting, showing no sign of involvement with anything that was going on around him. I carefully put a spoonful of rice into Mrs Hong's bowl, for which she thanked me, served Mrs Chen and Mr Chen, then bent over Yimou to reach his bowl. He beamed up at me, a face of pure innocence, turned towards his father and said, 'Pretty girl.'

Mr Chen gave a brief nod. Mrs Chen told him sweetly not to embarrass me. When I passed round the preserved meats, he beamed at me again, then leant across the table to whisper to Mrs Hong, 'Pretty girl, Grandma.'

'Eat your food, Yimou,' Mr Chen said sternly.

I disappeared back to the kitchen to fetch the hot dishes. The pieces of beef were stuck together in their glue-like sauce, the chicken was blackened in places where it had burnt at the bottom of the wok. I tried to disguise the worst with carefully positioned vegetables, but I knew that such subterfuge would not escape Mrs Chen's eagle eye. At least I had managed not to overcook the pakchoi. I carried the dishes through and waited for the inevitable smile-disguised tongue-lashing.

'You may serve us with more rice, then return to the kitchen to begin washing-up,' Mrs Chen ordered.

I filled one bowl after the other as before. When I reached Yimou, he suddenly pointed at my hand and said very solemnly, 'Nasty cut? Have to kiss it better.'

With that, he took hold of my wrist and was about to kiss my finger, when Mr Chen pulled him away and said firmly, 'No, Yimou, you don't touch.'

I was sent back to the kitchen then, while Yimou leaned across to Mrs Hong and whispered, 'Nasty cut, Grandma.'

I was in turmoil as I scrubbed away at the dirty pans. It wasn't that Mrs Chen would come in soon to demolish me over the dreadful meal. It was Yimou. It seemed I was destined to marry a boy who was as handsome as any girl could wish, but who acted like a very young child, though he looked about eighteen.

I didn't have time to think about it for too long. Mrs Chen strode in and the expected castigation took place. The food wasn't fit for a peasant. Mr Chen had been assured by my uncle that I was a good cook, so I had better not be there under false pretences. There was plenty left, which I was welcome to. Lunch had better be much improved. I was to make a start on it as soon as I had eaten and finished clearing up.

'One last thing, Lu Si-yan,' Mrs Chen said quietly. 'He is harmless, you will always have a roof over your head, and you will never want for money. I think you can count yourself lucky, don't you?'

I wanted to knock the sickly smile off her face and scream, No, no, no! I am not lucky. I am the unluckiest girl in the whole of China. But I wasn't expected to reply. Mrs Chen had already gone.

I fetched the bowls of discarded food from the dining room and sat down to eat, but I had lost my appetite. I didn't care about having a roof over my head – after all, Mother and I had managed without one once upon a time. I didn't care about money. We had never had money – not much, anyway. I remembered one of my father's favourite sayings: 'If you realise that you have enough, you are truly rich.' The Chens had more than enough money, but were they truly rich, Mr Chen with his empty eyes, Mrs Chen with her heart of stone?

I could see it all now. I was being trained to look after Yimou, to take over from Mrs Chen, and, as his wife, it would be much more difficult for me to leave him than if I were simply a paid servant.

I was in trouble again at lunchtime. I forgot the soup. The scolding missed its target this time though. I was too busy wondering if Yimou knew that I was to marry him. I caught him gazing at me adoringly, as small children sometimes do, and wished that I could just be friends with him.

By the evening, I was so tired that I could hardly keep my eyes open. Disaster struck when I managed to ladle soup into Mrs Hong's lap. Yimou burst out laughing, then clamped his hand over his mouth when he saw his father's face. Mrs Chen leapt to her feet, called me a stupid, clumsy child, and said that perhaps she was mistaken in thinking she could turn a sow's ear into a silk purse. Mrs Hong patted me on the back and told me not to worry, that it had been a long day.

'The poor child's exhausted,' she declared to Mr Chen. 'Let her have a bowl of food, then send her to her room. We can sort ourselves out here for once.'

Mr Chen nodded, but I knew from the look on Mrs Chen's face that she was furious again with her mother-in-law for interfering.

'The poor child's exhausted,' I heard Yimou repeat as I left the room.

'The poor child is being spoiled,' I heard Mrs Chen retort.

Chapter Seventeen
You Have Made Your Own Bed

The following week, Xiong Fei was dismissed. It was my fault. I told him nothing at first about what had happened on Sunday, except that my cooking had failed the test and that I had missed Mrs Hong's bowl and put her soup in her lap instead, which amused him greatly.

'Pity it wasn't Mrs Chen's lap,' he grinned. 'You need to improve your aim, Lu Si-yan.'

'If it had been Mrs Chen's lap, I might not have survived to tell the story. At least Mrs Hong was nice about it.'

'So what was the husband-to-be like?' Xiong Fei gazed at me searchingly.

'Very handsome,' I managed, after a pause, refusing

to meet his eye.

'Very handsome, but –?'

'Beautifully dressed.'

'Beautifully dressed, but –? Come on, Lu Si-yan, tell me. I'm your friend. All you've told me so far is that he's nicely packaged.'

I couldn't tell him. I feared that if I did, he would confront Mrs Chen. I didn't want that to happen. It was my problem, not Xiong Fei's.

'I can't really say,' I answered finally. 'I didn't see much of him. He didn't speak very much. He seemed – harmless enough.'

At the end of the week, though, I couldn't help blurting out how I felt. I had been woken very early that morning by my door opening and a figure standing there. It was Yimou, I could see from the spill of light from the hall. I heard him whispering, 'The poor child's exhausted. Kiss it better. Have to kiss it better.' I was petrified that he was going to come in and kiss my hand. I lay still, not daring to move in case it encouraged him to enter. Mr Chen came to my rescue again. As soon as Yimou heard his voice, he closed the door and went away.

Mrs Chen was particularly demanding that day. In the evening, Xiong Fei arrived to find me close to tears. When he asked me what was wrong, I told him of my fears that Yimou would come into my room. He was horrified.

'You said he was harmless, Lu Si-yan. How can you be so sure? He might be dangerous, for all you know.'

I tried to explain. 'He seems harmless because he's like a small child. He's never grown up, Xiong Fei. I think his brain is not quite right. He's harmless, but I'm frightened of him because I don't understand him.'

'How can you stay here and marry him then, Lu Si-yan?' Xiong Fei could see I was about to cry, and put his arms round me, just as Mrs Chen came into the kitchen. He let go of me instantly to plant himself in between Mrs Chen and me.

'What's going on?' demanded Mrs Chen. 'What are you doing?'

'I'm protecting Lu Si-yan from you, Mrs Chen,' Xiong Fei replied fiercely. 'Why do you treat her like a slave? Why are you forcing her to marry your son? What sort of people are you?'

Mrs Chen gaped in astonishment. In the silence that

followed Xiong Fei's outburst, time seemed to stand still. At last she found her voice, chilling in its wrath.

'How dare you! How dare you, a mere student, a mere nothing, criticise those of us who labour to feed and clothe you? You will finish making our meal, then you will leave, for good.'

'No, Mrs Chen,' Xiong Fei retorted, 'I will not finish making your meal. I am leaving now. I will not work for people who mercilessly exploit young children. I only hope that Lu Si-yan will find a way to escape your clutches. She deserves better.'

'Then you will leave without pay,' snarled Mrs Chen.

As he headed for the door, Xiong Fei turned and said, 'I'm sorry, Lu Si-yan. I will try to find help for you.' But even as he said it, I realised that there was nothing he could do. Mr and Mrs Chen were powerful people. They would know how to deal with anyone who questioned my status within their household.

Things deteriorated even more from that time onwards. Mrs Chen was incensed by what she considered the treachery of her pet chef and my role in his departure. She quickly replaced Xiong Fei with a much older man, who was under strict instructions to keep me in my place and only to talk to me, if necessary, to tell me what to do. Mr Tian, as I was to call him, clearly thought himself far too important anyway to speak to the likes of me, though he was not beyond pinching my bottom when the mood took him. When he arrived in the evenings, he often smelled of alcohol, and left mess all over the kitchen which he expected me to clean up.

Mrs Chen made me work harder than ever.

'You have made your own bed, Lu Si-yan – now you must lie in it. I have tried to treat you well, but you betrayed my goodwill. It is for you to prove to me that I can trust you again and that you can achieve the standards I expect of my future daughter-in-law.'

And so the weeks went by. I was allowed out of the apartment once a month to have my hair cut. The summer turned to autumn, then winter, but my only experience of the changing seasons was through the apartment windows. The river came and went, shrouded most of the time in dense smog, and screened too by heavy cloud or driving rain. I struggled to hang on to the idea that it might one day take me home.

No task was too menial. I disinfected toilets, scrubbed floors, cleaned windows, laundered underwear, ironed sheets, on top of my original kitchen and light house-work duties. I learned to get on with my work, to avoid any confrontation that might aggravate Mrs Chen still further.

I stopped looking in my bedroom mirror. The alien being who stood there was nobody I knew.

Sundays were the worst. The meals I cooked always failed to live up to Mrs Chen's high expectations, and Mr Tian made no effort to help me. On top of that, I didn't know how to deal with Yimou. He would gaze at me with fascination, as though I were some kind of rare species. He never spoke directly to me, but often talked about me in my presence. One day, he asked Mrs Chen if I could stay with them for ever and ever. Mrs Chen replied that that would be my decision, and glared at me tight-mouthed in case I should dare to contradict her.

Another day Yimou looked at me all glassy-eyed, then leant across the table to Mrs Hong and whispered, 'Don't tell anyone, Grandma, but I love Lu Si-yan. She is so beautiful. One day I will marry her and then she'll never, never, never go away.'

'Behave yourself, Yimou,' jumped in Mr Chen, while Mrs Chen gasped, and I stood there horrorstruck. Did

Yimou know? Did he know what was being planned for him?

'I think you have a fan there, Lu Si-yan,' smiled Mrs Hong. 'He has very good taste, I must say.'

'He has very good taste, hasn't he, Grandma?' Yimou nodded.

'That's enough,' thundered Mrs Chen. 'Stop encouraging him, Mother. He doesn't know what he's saying.'

'He doesn't know what he's saying,' repeated Yimou.

I disappeared back to the kitchen and sobbed.

Mrs Hong saw what was happening to me. Occasionally, at meal times, I would catch her look of consternation as she glanced in my direction.

'Are you sure you're not overworking this child?' she asked from time to time. Or, 'Lu Si-yan is looking very pale and thin. Perhaps she needs a few days' break.'

But, on seeing his wife's pursed lips, Mr Chen would reply, 'I'm sure my wife knows what she is doing, Mother. Please don't interfere.'

Mrs Chen rarely left me alone in the apartment with her mother-in-law. She would arrange for a carer to come in and look after Mrs Hong's needs whenever she went out. In that way, any contact with my sole sympa-thiser was kept to a minimum.

One day, though, Mrs Chen had to go into town unexpectedly and left the two of us alone.

Mrs Hong came to find me. She pressed some money into my hand.

'Take it, child. I know you're in training, but I think you should be paid something for all that you do, even if we feed and house you.'

I was astonished. I could feel tears pricking the backs of my eyes.

'Thank you, Mrs Hong. That's very kind of you.' Then, without thinking, I said, 'I shall send it to my mother.'

It was Mrs Hong's turn to be astonished.

'But your mother's dead, dear.'

I didn't know what to say then. I muttered something about being confused, and hoped Mrs Hong would go away. But instead she said, 'You're very unhappy here, aren't you, Lu Si-yan?'

She looked at me piercingly and continued, 'She can be a little hard, my daughter-in-law. She was devastated when she discovered that her one and only child was brain-damaged at birth. She has never come to terms with it, wants someone to blame, and is desperate for Yimou to be normal. Of course he won't ever be, but he's such a sweetheart. The trouble is, my daughter-in-law simply can't cope with the burden of him.'

She stopped herself then and tutted. 'You are only a child, and I am speaking out of turn like old women do sometimes, but I hope that by understanding her pain you will judge her less harshly.'

'I miss my home,' I said.

'Come, I will make you tea and you shall tell me about your home.'

Mrs Hong sent me to sit down in her room. I didn't protest, I needed so much just to do nothing for a few minutes. I hadn't the energy to worry about Mrs Chen's reaction were she to find out.

'Where does Yimou go during the day?' I asked, when Mrs Hong returned with a tray full of tea and cakes.

'He works for his father. Simple jobs that keep him busy and make him feel important.'

I nodded, wondering again if this was the moment to let Mrs Hong know of the plans being made for me.

'You are full of unspoken thoughts, Lu Si-yan. Tell me

about your family.'

So I told her. About Father and his love of life, the way he sang as he worked, about the carp we caught, about how I taught him to read, and how he was taken from us in a road accident. I told her about Li-hu with his rosy cheeks and how, when Father died, I helped to look after him and he helped to collect the eggs from our ducks and hens. I told her about Uncle, and how I didn't think he really approved of us, but he had had a difficult time when he was young because he had had to bring up my father. I told her about my mother, and how hard it had been for her when Father died, but how we had become an inseparable team and had managed really well, until she became ill and there was a terrible drought and everything went wrong.

Tears rolled down my face as all the memories came flooding back. I wanted my mother. I wanted Li-hu. I no longer blamed him for my plight. How could I? He was just a baby. He didn't ask for this to happen. Mrs Hong looked at me pityingly.

'What happened to your little brother, Lu Si-yan?' she asked, patting me on the hand. 'Is your uncle look-ing after him?'

'I don't know,' I sobbed. 'But one day I will go home and find him.'

'Would you like me to write to your uncle?'

I shook my head. 'I don't want to be a burden to my family. I will go home when I am able to support them myself.'

'That will be soon, Lu Si-yan, I promise. You are learning fast, and your resilience will see you through.'

Chapter Eighteen
You Have to Leave

One evening, when I had retired to my room and was on the verge of falling asleep, a furious row erupted in the apartment. I crept over to my door and tried to make out what was going on, but the voices were too muffled. Intrigued, I opened the door slightly, and heard my name spoken by Mr Chen. I heard Mrs Hong arguing with him, saying that she wouldn't allow him to do it if that was what they were planning, that it was wrong, that she couldn't believe that a son of hers would behave in such a way. I heard Mrs Chen telling her to be quiet and to mind her own business. Mrs Hong retorted that it was very much her business and that her daughter-in-law should learn some respect. Mr Chen told her firmly that it was not her place to interfere and that she must leave the subject alone. His words were final. A door slammed. I scuttled back to bed.

Several days later, Mrs Chen went out and left a carer in charge of Mrs Hong. I went about my duties as usual. Before very long, though, I heard the apartment door open and close, and Mrs Hong's wheelchair approaching. She came into the kitchen and said, 'That's got rid of her. Now, Lu Si-yan, put down that saucepan and listen.'

I did as I was told.

'My daughter-in-law might take me for an old fool, but I'm not senile yet. I have finally got to the bottom of what is going on here, Lu Si-yan, and I am appalled. It's wrong. My son and daughter-in-law, however, seem determined to ignore my views. But I won't let it happen. You have to leave. You have to leave now.'

I stared at her in amazement, unable to take in what she meant.

'We haven't much time, child,' continued Mrs Hong. 'My daughter-in-law may be back at any moment.'

She reached into the handbag on her lap and pulled out a purse. 'I want you to take this. There should be enough to get you home and quite a bit to spare for your family.'

I hesitated. How could I take this kindly old lady's money?

'Don't argue, Lu Si-yan. I am well looked after, even if they do treat me like an invalid. I want you to have it. It's the least I can do to make up for my family's behaviour. Now run and collect your things together.'

I hesitated again, then took the purse from her and ran to my room. I grabbed my old blouse from behind the chest of drawers and piled my clothes into a carrier bag. My coat was hanging on the back of my door. Should I take it? Wouldn't it be stealing? It would be cold outside though, and all I was wearing was my servant's dress. I put the coat on and walked back to the kitchen. The enormity of what I was about to do made me shudder with apprehension.

Mrs Hong held her arms open and beckoned me towards her. I went to her and hugged her tight.

'Go home, Lu Si-yan,' she said. 'Go and find that brother of yours.'

'And my mother,' I said.

'But your mother –' Mrs Hong began.

'My mother is alive, Mrs Hong. I am not an orphan. Only my father is dead.'

The old lady's face flashed anger, followed by despair. 'Then go to your mother. She must be missing you terribly. Give me your address and I will tell her to expect you.'

I quickly wrote it down, while Mrs Hong wheeled herself to the apartment door, took a key from her bag, and opened it.

'Good luck, Lu Si-yan. Remember me sometimes.'

'I will, Mrs Hong, and thank you.'

Chapter Nineteen
What's Gone is Gone

I ran down the twenty-two flights of steps, too fearful to take the lift in case Mrs Chen should arrive back unexpectedly and catch me in it. When I reached the front door, I checked carefully that no one was watching, slipped out on to the busy street and mingled with a passing group of pedestrians. The freezing air shocked me. It was the middle of winter. The dense, dull, grey sky threatened snow. I was glad I had taken the coat Mrs Chen had bought me, though what a waste of money it had proved until now.

I turned into the first side road I came to. Initially on a level, leading me back behind the row of new apartment blocks where the Chens lived, this road suddenly dropped steeply and took me towards the derelict buildings I had seen from my bedroom window. I glanced back up at the new apartments, trying to work out which one was the Chens', hoping to wave one final farewell to Mrs Hong. But the windows were all blank canvases.

As I drew nearer to the derelict buildings, I was surprised to see that though they were appallingly dirty and crumbling, several of them were still occupied, their balconies hung with washing and cluttered with bicycles, tin baths, old stoves and other worldly possessions. A grubby-faced little girl waved at me from one of the higher balconies. I waved back and thought how lucky I was to have grown up with my father's luscious green terraces all around me, with fresh eggs every day, with the river running close by, and the air clean and transparent.

The road petered out. I turned right along another decaying street, and was surprised this time to find a row of shops, their owners trading as though nothing was happening around them and the new town above didn't exist. Was the attraction of a brand new apartment, a brand new shop, insufficient to tear them away from this squalor?

Yet how could I even ask myself such a question? This

was where their roots were, this was their home. I was looking at these people through the eyes of someone who had lived in a luxurious apartment for the past four months, and some of that must have rubbed off on me. I knew that I would not have questioned their decision to stay, nor even noticed the squalor, before I had been exposed to the Chens' immaculate lifestyle.

I walked faster, partly because of the sense of freedom I began to feel, partly because I did not want to attract too much attention. I turned down a quiet, narrow alleyway to continue my descent towards the river. Shortly, I came to the wasteland that had lain grey and melancholy as a backdrop to my bedroom panorama. The scale of it took my breath away. To the right and left, for as far as I could see, there was nothing but pile upon pile of dust-smothered rubble, the odd twisted pipe sticking up through it as though searching for a vital puff of air. I started to pick my way across it, my progress slowed by the unevenness of the ground. Looking at the rubble more closely, in order to avoid treading in potholes or cutting myself on jagged edges, I spotted tiny fragments of the lives that were once lived where I now stood. A doll's head, a strip of blue material, an old shoe, a broken bowl. Ahead of me, I saw a man and a woman pulling at the rubble with their hands as though they were looking for something. Had they lived there once? I wondered if they had left some indispensable part of their lives behind them and were now engaged in a frantic search to find it. Or were they simply hoping to find treasure amongst the fallen landmarks of somebody else's life?

I reached a path and quickened my pace again. It narrowed and began to slope abruptly. I followed its meandering line with my eyes. It led all the way down to the river, where a ferry was moored and dozens of people were milling around. My heart skipped a beat. Nearly there. Freedom just a few hundred yards away.

I broke into a jog. The path gave way to coarse grass on either side. Ahead of me, the ferry passengers were strung out along the path, large bundles tied to their backs. I realised that they were coming in my direction, that the crowd by the ferry had disappeared. I saw then that the ferry was moving away. Even as I realised that I had missed it, I kept running towards it in some vague hope that it might stop.

''Fraid you're too late, dear,' the first man I reached

said. 'There won't be another one till morning now.'

'But there's got to be,' I replied. 'Are you sure?'

'Seven o'clock tomorrow morning's the next one. Nothing till then.'

The straggle of climbers passed me one by one as I stood in the middle of the path gazing in utter dismay at the departing ferry. What was I to do? By now the Chens might well be scouring the streets of the old town for me. It was late afternoon. Where could I go until the morning?

The last of the ferry passengers walked by, several of them staring at me curiously. I hurried down the path and waited for them to disappear along the streets behind me. To the left of the path, some hundred yards away, the remains of a small dwelling protruded through the grass. When I was sure nobody was looking, I scrambled over to it. The stubs of the walls were just high enough, if I lay down, to screen me from the path and protect me from the bitter wind. I decided to stay there until darkness fell, then to find somewhere in the old town to spend the night.

With my coat wrapped tightly around me and my bag clutched in my hand, despite my fear of being found and the constant noise from boats labouring along the river, I fell asleep.

It was twilight by the time I woke again. The surrounding peace was punctuated every so often by warning sirens from somewhere along the river, but otherwise all was quiet. I left the safety of my hideout and made my way back up the path through the wasteland towards the old town. As I drew closer, I could see that the shop-lined street was still busy with people fetching last-minute provisions, chatting with friends, playing cards, eating meals at pavement tables, the heat from ash-filled grill cookers keeping them warm. Although I was hungry by now, I dared not stop to buy food, nor to thaw my frozen fingers. I slipped quickly past the end of the street, and kept going until I found a whole row of deserted apartment blocks. The door of one of them was partially open. I pushed it hard to make enough room to squeeze through, listened for any sound that might mean it was occupied, then ran up the stairs right to the top floor and into a room at the front.

A meagre thread of light penetrated through the cracked windows. The room was bare apart from a filthy blanket in one corner, a pile of old electrical wire in another, and a scattering of litter across the floor. It's only for one night, I told myself. I sat down on the broken floorboards with my back against a wall. I was too scared and too cold to go to sleep. I kept hearing unfamiliar noises: creaks and scratches and rasps and whines. I prayed that there were no rats around. Surely they wouldn't climb that high. Part of me began to long for the comfortable bed in my room at the Chens', but I reproached myself for even thinking that I wanted to go back.

Then I heard footsteps on the stairs. Two sets. Men's voices. I grabbed the filthy blanket and pulled it over me in terror. I shrank into the corner, hoping that if I made myself as small as possible I wouldn't be noticed. The footsteps kept on coming. The voices grew louder. They were outside the room. I heard a door creak, then close. The voices immediately became muffled. The two men had gone into the room opposite and closed the door behind them.

It was stifling under the foul-smelling blanket. I lifted it away from my face, only to be teased by the smell of food. The men were obviously eating next door. I could hear music too. I was desperate for them to leave. Why couldn't they have chosen one of the other apartment blocks? Why mine? They were probably regular visitors. I wondered whether to steal out of the building while they had their door closed, but it was dark outside now, as well as freezing cold, and I was too scared to move in case they heard me. I could only hope that they would leave me alone in my room while they remained locked in theirs.

After perhaps an hour, maybe two hours, the voices and the music stopped. I was struggling to keep my eyes open, but I stayed awake for another half an hour or so, before deciding that the two men must be asleep and that I was safe at least for a while. I lay down, pulled the collar of my coat round my ears, wrapped the blanket round the lower part of my body and hid my bag under it as well, then fell asleep myself.

I woke again at dawn, stiff with cold and ravenous. All was quiet in the building. The ferry would leave, I judged, in about an hour. I had to be on it. I couldn't stay here another day and night, but how would I know whether it was safe to leave? I decided that the only thing I could do would be to make a dash for it. I waited for another nerve-wracking stretch of time. There was still no sound from the room across the hall. I stood up quietly and stretched my legs, picked up my bag, then moved silently towards the door. I peered round it and my heart skipped a beat. The door opposite was open. I listened hard. Not a sound. The men must have gone already. I took a deep breath, leapt out into the hallway, then belted down the stairs, two at a time, and out through the front door.

It had snowed during the night. A sprinkling covered the ground, smoothing its jagged edges and bleaching the greyness from the landscape. The murky sky suggested there was more to come. I hurried down the path, joining a steady stream of people who were also heading for the river. Their early-morning chatter cheered me, a sense of excitement eclipsed my fears.

As I drew closer to the waiting ferry, I scoured the quayside for the Chens, but saw no one of their grandeur. I mingled with a large group of women who, it appeared from their conversation, were on their way to work at a factory further down the river, and boarded the ferry with them. It seemed an eternity before the engines started up, but at last they roared into action. The horn sounded, and we moved slowly, slowly away from the landing stage, away from a period of my life I was only too happy to leave behind.

The ferry picked up speed. I breathed a sigh of relief. I was safe at last. I would stay on the ferry for as long as possible, then make my way home somehow or other, by bus or by train. It couldn't be that difficult, I thought, to work out a route back. I stood by the edge and gazed over to the far side of the river, where buildings lower down had been obliterated and smallholdings abandoned. Higher up, another new town stood proud.

'Lucky people, aren't they?'

A rather overweight man had come to stand next to me. I looked at him, bewildered. He pointed across the water.

'Nice new homes they've got now. New jobs too, most of them. Nice warm factories instead of having to break their backs digging for a pittance.'

I didn't think my family would have agreed. Father had always refused to work in a factory, however much Uncle had tried to persuade him. I didn't want to talk to this man, though. I just wanted to be alone with my thoughts.

'Are you going far?' he asked.

I nodded but made no effort to continue the conversation, hoping he'd go away.

'Bit young to be on your own, aren't you?'

'I'm older than I look,' I said, trying to sound tough.

'Old enough to work?' he continued. 'My wife and I, we're always on the lookout for girls to work in our factories. You won't find better.'

'I don't want to work in a factory,' I said. 'I'm going home.'

'That's our loss, then,' said the man. 'I hope you have a good journey.' He flashed me a smile before turning away.

I was relieved that at that moment the ticket man approached me.

'Where to, Miss?' he asked.

'All the way, please.'

He told me how much I had to pay and I reached into my bag to take out the money. I delved down to the bottom, my fingers itching to touch the fat wad of crisp notes Mrs Hong had given me. I couldn't find it. I could feel my face turning red, my heart thumping. I searched around with my hand, then opened the bag wider and pulled out my clothes to look underneath. The money wasn't there.

'Got a problem, Miss?' asked the ticket man.

'My money – it's gone. Someone's taken my money,' I wailed. It hit me like a sledgehammer, the awful realisation that it must have been the men I had heard in the night. I knew something had been wrong that morning. It was the pile of electrical wire. It had gone. The men had come into my room for the wire. They had discovered me sound asleep. They had found my bag and stolen my money.

I must have fainted at the thought of it, for the next thing I knew I was sitting on the floor of the ferry being comforted by a tiny woman.

'Don't you worry, my darling,' said the woman. 'I've paid your fare. You just sit there until you feel better.'

'But the money,' I sobbed, as I realised again what had happened. 'I need it to get home. My mother's expecting me.'

'What a terrible stroke of luck you've suffered, but I'm afraid there's no use crying,' said the woman, not unkindly. 'What's gone is gone.'

I hauled myself to my feet, aware of the pitying stares of the other passengers.

'You don't understand,' I sobbed again. 'I need it for

my mother. I can't go home without it.'

'That bad, eh?' sympathised the woman. 'I wonder if there's anything my husband and I can do to help you.'

She called across the boat, and the fat man who had spoken to me earlier came over to us.

'This young lady's had her money stolen, poor thing,' she said to him. 'And there she was saving it to help her poor mother.'

'I don't know what the world's coming to,' said the man. 'It's always the good folk who get taken advantage of.'

'We can help her though, can't we?' urged the woman. 'Help her earn some money for her family.'

'Like I told her, we employ a lot of young girls in our factories,' said the man, 'but she doesn't want to work in a factory, so I'm afraid we can't really help.'

'Oh, but it's good pay, my dear,' the woman encouraged. 'Good pay. Good conditions. You come with us and you'll earn enough in no time.'

'You work hard enough,' said the man, 'and we'll have you home for Spring Festival. Plenty of young ladies would jump at the chance, but you must make up your own mind.'

Spring Festival. A month away. I could cope with that, couldn't I, after all I had been through? My heart skipped at the thought of how my mother's face would look if I walked through the door in time for Spring Festival, in time to give her a fistful of money to spend on our celebrations.

'What sort of factory?' I asked.

'The best,' said the man. 'A toy factory.'

'Dolls, teddy bears, furry animals, rubber ducks, plastic lorries. Everything,' enthused the woman. 'Lots of other young girls work there.'

Perhaps they would let me take something back for Li-hu, I smiled to myself.

'We're Mr and Mrs Wang.' The woman held out her hand. 'Trust us, my dear. We'll see you're all right.'

'I'm Lu Si-yan,' I said, shyly, shaking first her hand and then his. 'Thank you for your help.'

Mr and Mrs Wang shared some food with me and asked me about myself. I told them a little about my family, but when they began to pry into my recent past, I said that I had worked as a domestic, and left it at that. They seemed friendly enough, but I was worried at the thought that I was putting my well-being into the hands of complete strangers, and I instinctively felt that the less they knew about me the better. I had no choice but to trust them, though. They were offering me a lifeline.

Chapter Twenty
Only the Best

We left the ferry more than a dozen stops further on, by which time it was nearly midday. As soon as we were ashore, Mr Wang hailed a taxi. We were taken up a steep hill, through another partially demolished, deserted old town, beyond the new town above it, and out into the country, leaving the river far behind us. We travelled for several miles before we reached a small, shabby industrial town, where factory after factory belched foul-smelling smoke into the atmosphere, and where row upon row of concrete dormitories lined the roads. We pulled up outside the gates of one of the factories.

'Here we are,' said Mr Wang proudly. 'All this belongs to us. This factory and the two alongside. Three factories, three hundred workers.'

'And you will be one of them, Lu Si-yan,' added Mrs Wang brightly.

I looked at the grimy, featureless facade of the building, its windows tiny and too dirty to see through. Yellow smoke poured from its eight chimneys, otherwise there was no sign of life from the outside. Mr Wang unlocked the gates. We walked round to a side door, along a short, neon-lit corridor and into his office. A huge black desk dominated the room, which was decorated with an assortment of garish paintings, a red and gold silk carpet and an enormous red sofa.

Mr Wang plumped himself down at the desk. Very quickly he told me how much I would be paid and when, what hours I would work, and what I would earn if I worked extra hours.

'We're very generous with our overtime payments,' he said.

'Very generous,' echoed Mrs Wang.

It sounded like a fortune, for I had never earned money before. If I worked lots of extra hours I was sure I could leave after a month and be home, as Mr Wang had said, in time for the Spring Festival. That was all I could think of then, just getting through whatever the work entailed, and handing my wages to my mother.

'You'll sleep in one of our dormitories with some of the other girls,' continued Mr Wang.

'It's very cosy and I'm sure you'll make lots of friends,' said Mrs Wang.

'And you'll be fed on the premises. We pay for that ourselves.' Mr Wang patted his paunch.

'It's good food, too,' smiled Mrs Wang. 'Only the best for our workers.'

'Off you go, then. Remember, work hard and you'll reap the rewards.' Mr Wang dismissed me with a wave of the hand.

'Come with me, dear,' said Mrs Wang. 'We'll look after your nice coat for you and get you kitted out like the other girls. We provide you with two sets of overalls which you must wear all the time and wash yourself.'

She took me along another corridor, into a changing room. From a cupboard, she pulled out some overalls and made me put them on instead of the clothes I was wearing. They were far too big, but Mrs Wang looked at me and nodded approvingly.

'Perfect,' she said. 'Now, keep your own clothes with you and you can put them in a locker in your dormitory later on. One of the girls will find you a space.'

She led me from the room and down another corridor. 'Can you sew?' she asked.

I nodded, grimacing inwardly as I remembered the last time I had been asked that question.

'Then how would you like to make teddy bears? We've got lots of orders for those at the moment, so we could do with an extra pair of hands on the production line.'

I nodded again.

'Good.' Mrs Wang clapped her hands. 'Come on, then. I'll show you where to go and find out what you'll be doing.'

She led me down another corridor to a door at the end. She opened the door, pulled me through and shut it quickly behind her. The wave of heat made me gasp. The smell of stale air was nauseating. In front of me, rows of young women and girls were hunched over sewing machines. Not one of them looked up when we came in. Mrs Wang walked me between two of the rows to the far side of the room, where a supervisor sat watching the girls.

'Mrs Li, this is our new recruit, Lu Si-yan,' said Mrs

Wang. 'Where would you like her?'

'Eyes,' Mrs Li replied, looking at me sourly. 'A little young, isn't she?'

'Fifteen, and eager to do as much work as possible, aren't you, dear?' Mrs Wang answered quickly, staring at me for confirmation, though we hadn't discussed my age. I lowered my head in a half-nod.

'Will her hands do?' asked the supervisor.

'I'm sure they'll harden up in no time,' smiled Mrs Wang. 'I'll leave her to you.'

Mrs Wang disappeared back through the room and out through the door. The supervisor rose reluctantly from her table.

'This way, then,' she said, without looking at me.

I followed her to the end of a row, where she made a young woman stop what she was doing and move to another position. She sat me down at the vacated table and picked up a faceless bear from a box on the floor.

'This is all you have to do,' she said, pulling a carton of glass eyes towards her and taking two. 'Poke two small holes where the eyes are to go. Tie each eye into the middle of a strand of upholstery thread. Squeeze the eye wires together to form a pin. Ease the threads on to a needle. Push the needle into the eyehole and pull the threads gently to work the wires into the eyehole to seat the eye.'

She continued apace, without checking to see that I understood her instructions, until both eyes were in place. It was amusing to see the bear's face begin to come to life, but I was anxious that I should find the procedure too difficult. I wished I could start with the nose, which I was sure would be much easier. The supervisor stood up and told me to sit down.

'You will have the rest of today to practise,' she said expressionlessly. 'You are lucky this is the quiet season. You will be expected to keep up with the rest of the girls. We do not tolerate slackness.'

She indicated that I should practise on the bears in the box, then returned to the far side of the room without another word. I peered round to see if anyone was looking at me, but the girls were all too busy concentrating on their own bit of bear-making. I pulled a bear out of the box, two eyes from the carton, and tried to remember what I had to do. Poking the holes, which had seemed the simplest part of the operation, proved to be the first difficulty. I ended up with one much higher than the other, giving the bear a rather mischievous look once the eyes were in place. Threading the needle and pushing it through the dense stuffing and coarse-lined fur was the next major hurdle. I rammed it as hard as I could, joggling it around, but achieved no more than a shallow indentation. I tried again and again, my fingers growing redder and redder, perspiration pouring down my face.

I looked to either side of me for help. The girl to my left stole a glance in my direction and whispered, 'Use the needle-grabber.'

I had no idea what a needle-grabber was, but she pointed to a piece of leather on my table, then returned to her work.

'Thanks,' I whispered, but she made no acknowledgement.

I wrapped the needle in the leather and tried again to push it through the bear's head. It still refused to budge at first. With perseverance, though, I finally managed to work the needle out through the bear's neck. I breathed a sigh of relief and stretched my arms out, only to catch the disapproving look of the supervisor. I pulled hard on the threads to manoeuvre the eye into position, and was pleased that it actually stayed put, even if it was a little too low.

I set to work on the second eye. I managed to push the needle through more quickly this time, but when it came to tying the threads together, they cut painfully into my fingers. I couldn't believe that making a bear could be so difficult.

At last, the two eyes were in place. I stood the bear up in front of me and couldn't help smiling at his cock-eyed look. I wished I could keep him. I traced with my finger where I would have sewn his nose and a big smiley mouth. I would have called him One Eye Up, One Eye Down Bear, I decided, were I allowed to keep him.

'You'll have to speed up if you want to keep your job here.' The supervisor's acid voice cut through my reverie. 'Two eyes are not much to show for over an hour's work. Two eyes that are far from straight.'

'It's making my hands sore,' I said, hoping that she might move me to noses or paws.

'It's the same for everyone when they start. You just have to get used to it.'

The supervisor returned to her seat. I picked up another bear and began the same process again, making sure this time that the eyeholes were in alignment. For the rest of the afternoon, I threaded and shoved and jiggled and pulled until my shoulders ached and my hands were stiff and bloody. Yet I managed to complete only four bears. Each time, the stuffing resisted my most strenuous efforts to push the needle through it. I couldn't see how I was ever going to speed up, and the threat that I might lose my job petrified me.

A bell sounded. The other girls stopped what they were doing immediately and dashed for the door. I wasn't sure whether I should follow or wait for the supervisor to tell me what to do, but then I saw that she was disappearing just as quickly. The girl who had spoken to me previously told me to hurry up.

'Aren't you hungry?' she asked. 'It's suppertime.'

I dropped my work and jumped to my feet. I followed her along another corridor, through a door to the outside, and across a concrete courtyard towards one of two enormous corrugated iron buildings, where dozens of other workers were converging. We piled through the doors into a cavernous canteen furnished with endless lines of large round plastic tables and chairs. The tables were covered with metal tureens of steaming food.

I kept close to the girl who had befriended me and sat down next to her, hoping she wouldn't mind. She took a plastic bowl from a pile in the middle and served herself from one of the tureens. As I did the same, she warned, 'Be sure to eat well, but don't take more than you can manage. They'll fine you if you leave any.'

I nodded, grateful but shocked at what she had said, though I was so hungry that I was sure I would have been able to eat anything that was put before me. However, my appetite quickly disappeared as I tried my first mouthful of the chewy, over-salted meat stew that was our dinner. For the second time since I had run away, I found I was imagining myself back at the Chens', where the food had always been delicious, even if I was only given leftovers. Everyone around me was tucking in voraciously. Were they used to the food, no longer noticing its awfulness? Were they hungrier than me? Or had they simply never tasted anything better? How strange, I thought, that regardless of how dreadful my time with the Chens had been, it had opened my eyes to how good some things in life could be. I steeled myself and swallowed the remains of the food in my bowl, washed down with a cup of thin, tepid tea.

'Are you sure you've had enough?' said the girl next to me. 'You need it to keep you going.'

'I've had plenty,' I said. 'What do we do now? Can we go to our rooms?'

The girl shook her head. 'Not yet. We go back to work. There's overtime for another four hours. Compulsory overtime.'

I could feel myself beginning to shake. Another four hours. I couldn't cope with another four hours. Not today. Not any day.

'Are you all right? You get used to it, you know. Sort of. What's your name?'

'Lu Si-yan,' I whispered.

'My name is Li Mei. Don't think me rude, but you look too young to be working.'

'I didn't think it would be like this, working in a factory. They made it sound so special.'

'They would. That's how they tempt people like us, people with no hope of anything better. I've been here for six months. Another six months and I'll leave and take the money I've saved back to my family. Is that why you're here?'

I nodded. 'I thought if I could just do a month. They

promised that would be enough. But I don't think I can even last a week.'

Li Mei gazed at me in consternation. 'How old are you, Lu Si-yan?' she asked.

'Nearly twelve,' I muttered.

The bell rang at that moment. Everyone stood up and headed quickly for the doors. Li Mei helped me to my feet.

'Think of your family, Lu Si-yan. Remember their faces, remember their smiles, remember the good times. Think of them and you'll get through.'

I nodded, but just the mention of my family made me want to cry my heart out. We hurried back across the courtyard. Li Mei squeezed my hand encouragingly when we re-entered the machine room. I sat down at my table, picked up a bear, kept my head bowed and struggled to regain my composure.

'You can do it,' whispered Li Mei.

I wished I could believe it. My hands were so sore that I could scarcely hold the needle, let alone exert enough pressure to push it through. The supervisor came and stood behind me.

'I knew it,' she growled, after watching me for several

minutes. 'Why do they give me these girls who are not up to the job?'

'Why don't I change with her?' Li Mei smiled at the supervisor. 'I'm good at eyes. Lu Si-yan can sew on the ears instead of me.'

I glanced gratefully at Li Mei, then stared straight ahead of me, certain that the supervisor would say no just to spite me. After what seemed like an eternity, she replied, 'She had better be good at ears. We are not running a charity here.'

She left Li Mei to show me what to do.

By the time the final bell rang, at half past ten, I was so exhausted that I could barely keep my eyes open. Even though it had been easier to sew on the ears, my hands were still bruised and bloody from pushing the needle through several layers of fur. My back and shoulders had begun to protest at every effort. But at least the supervisor had grudgingly accepted that I was better at ears than eyes and might make the grade in a week or so.

Li Mei took me under her wing and told the supervisor that there was space for me in her dormitory and that she would show me where to go and what to do. I was so relieved, for I was dreading having to sleep in a room full of strangers.

There were twenty beds crammed into our small dormitory. Five of them weren't yet being used because the busy season hadn't quite started at the factory. I chose the spare bed closest to Li Mei's. Like all the others, it was covered with a faded red blanket, there was a skinny pillow and at the end was a worn, discoloured towel. By the side of the bed was a small locker, into which I bundled my clothes and my bag.

Li Mei took me through to the washrooms. There were two basins and two showers to be shared by all of us. By the time we arrived, a queue had already formed outside the shower cubicle doors.

'It's always like this,' said Li Mei, grimacing. 'We have to wash our overalls in the basins or showers as well as ourselves. By the time we get to bed, it's almost time to get up again.'

'What time do we get up?' I asked, alarmed.

'Up at seven o'clock, start work at eight.'

Well, I was up at six o'clock at the Chens', I thought to myself, so seven o'clock wasn't so bad.

We joined the queue, though I was so desperate to go

to sleep that I would have been happy to go to bed as I was. While we waited, Li Mei introduced me to some of the other girls. They were all teenagers, I guessed, and I was by far the youngest. They laughed and joked as we stood there, relieved to be freed from the monotony of their individual tasks and the harsh regime of the work-room, even though they too were exhausted. I gathered that most of them would leave when they had made enough money, that they were never paid what they thought they were owed, that Mr Wang broke the law in forcing them to do overtime, that the supervisor told tales and was not to be trusted, and that from March onwards they would be working even longer hours to keep up with orders for Christmas toys from companies in other coun-tries. I was so glad that by then I would have left.

Tired as I was, I found it difficult to sleep that night. The hard, unfamiliar bed, the relentless wheezes and snorts of the fifteen other girls, my fear that I would be unable to cope with a full day's work the next day and that I would be thrown out on to the street, all con-tributed to hours spent tossing and turning in the dark. I finally dropped off, only to be woken what seemed like minutes later by the wake-up bell.

Chapter Twenty-one
Just Like Family

Without the friendship of the girls and Li Mei's protectiveness, I should never have survived those first few days. I dragged myself from my bed each morning, not the slightest bit rested and longing to crawl back under the covers. My back, neck and shoulders ached constantly from sitting in the same position all day long. My fingers became so tender it was agony using the needle. My head throbbed under the blazing fluorescent lights and at times my eyes became blurred. The initial relief at being put on to ears was short-lived, to be replaced by despair at the tedium of the task.

It was the same for all of us, though. We lived for the bells that signalled a ten-minute break in the morning, half an hour at lunchtime, ten minutes in the afternoon, forty minutes at dinnertime and, most of all, the bell that told us the day was over.

By the end of my third day, I had speeded up a lot, but I knew that I still had some way to go before the supervisor would be satisfied. Mrs Wang came to see me, looked at my work and said that I was doing well.

'Just ask for a meeting with me, dear, if you have any problems,' she said. 'We want you to be happy here. Our workers are just like family to us.'

In the dormitory that evening, the other girls imitated her.

'We want you to be happy here,' one of the girls said fawningly. 'Put up your hands if you're happy.'

They all sat on their hands, then fell about laughing.

'Our workers are just like family to us,' mocked another. 'Slaves, more like. How can she keep a straight face when she says such things?'

On Friday we had to present ourselves at Mr Wang's office, one by one, to receive our wages. I had no idea how much I was due, but with all the overtime I had worked, I was sure it must be a fair amount. I was excited at the prospect of coming away with my first sum of money towards the cost of my journey home and helping my mother. As I queued with the other girls, I couldn't wait for it to be my turn.

I was summoned at last. I knocked on Mr Wang's door and he called for me to enter and sit down.

'Doing reasonably well, I hear,' he said. 'Not up to scratch yet, but coming on. Of course, we don't pay you while you're training, and there's the little matter of the fare to repay, but we feed you for free and provide you with accommodation. If you carry on the way you are, young lady, then I shall be only too happy to hand over your first wage packet at the end of next week. I can't say fairer than that, can I? Now, be a good girl and close the door behind you, would you.'

I felt faint. I stood up as though in a trance. I don't know how I made it to the door, but as soon as I was out in the corridor I collapsed. The girls who were still in the queue gathered round me. Mr Wang, hearing the commotion, opened his door and told two of them to take me to the dormitory.

'She's not ill, I hope,' he said. 'Can't afford to employ people who keep fainting.'

When we reached the dormitory, I had recovered enough to send the girls away. They had their own wages to collect, and they were expected back at work.

Besides, I was desperate to be alone, to think things through, to come to some decision about what I was going to do. But, once again, what choice did I have? None, and the Wangs knew it. 'You work hard enough and we'll have you home for Spring Festival,' Mr Wang had said. Well, I had worked, and I had earned precisely nothing. A whole week had gone by. Only three weeks left now and I was no better off. I lay on my bed, ignored the bell for dinner and, in the rare moment of quiet, fell asleep.

I was woken when the girls came back to the dormitory just after half past ten. Li Mei sat on my bed, asked if I was all right, and held out a bowl of cold noodles for me.

'Eat, Lu Si-yan. I stole these for you. You must eat to keep up your strength. Anyway, they're the best thing we've had all week,' she smiled.

I took the bowl and thanked her. I hadn't realised how hungry I was, but until then I had only picked at the uniformly grey dishes that had been put before us morning, noon and night.

'Was it the wages?' asked Li Mei. 'Did they pay you too little?'

'They didn't pay me anything,' I muttered between

mouthfuls, almost ashamed to admit that the Wangs didn't think I was worth paying.

'Why, the tight-fisted, penny-pinching –' Li Mei was furious. 'They never pay what we think we're due, but it's despicable not to pay you at all. They're just taking advantage of you because of your age.'

'They said I'm in training and should be grateful for the free food and lodging.'

'Very grateful,' said Li Mei sarcastically. Then she turned to the others. 'Come on, girls,' she called. 'Let's have a whip-round for Lu Si-yan.'

I saw instantly that one or two of the girls were opposed to the idea. I leapt to my feet, red with embarrassment. 'No, please don't. You're very kind, but please don't. Mr Wang is sure I will have earned my money next week.'

Li Mei looked at me doubtfully, but didn't argue. The next morning, however, I found a small amount of money in my locker. I challenged Li Mei about it, but she denied all knowledge.

'Whoever gave it to you wants you to have it and will be offended if you don't accept it,' she said. 'And when we go into town tomorrow you will need some money.'

She saw the puzzlement on my face.

'It's Sunday tomorrow, and Sunday is our day off! Didn't they tell you? We sleep, Lu Si-yan, oh, how we sleep. Like babies in their mothers' arms. Breakfast isn't until half past nine. After that we have to wash our overalls and clean the dormitory, but then we're free to do as we like.'

'Ice cream, here we come,' cheered Song Shuru.

'Karaoke, here we come,' called Shen Enqing.

'Boys, here we come,' laughed Dong Ying, and they all began to chatter excitedly.

Saturday crawled past after that. The thought of no wake-up bell, the thought of no ears to sew, the thought of going into town with my new friends filled me with impatience. I glanced up at the clock in the workroom over and over again, willing the hands to move round more quickly. Once, the supervisor warned me about slacking, but even she couldn't dampen my spirit. For the first time since I had left home, I was being given the freedom to go out without fear, and to have fun. As for the possibility of meeting with boys, the idea made me feel incredibly adult and like a timid little girl all at the same time. How would I know what to say? I wondered.

I pushed the little girl aside. I was growing up fast and I wanted to be accepted by my friends as one of them.

At last, the final bell sounded. We all tore out of the workroom and into our dormitory. Several of the girls leapt out of their overalls and cavorted round the room, swinging their clothes over their heads before hurling them to the ground and jumping on them. Others threw themselves on to their beds. Dong Ying and Song Shuru started a pillow fight. Their screams of delight were infectious. Soon, all of us joined in. Even when one of the pillows burst, sending feathers flying all over the room, we carried on.

Then Li Mei began to sing, and we all stopped to listen. Shen Enqing sang in harmony with her, a beautiful song about mist and mountains, rivers and waterfalls, a cormorant fisherman sailing quietly along in the golden light of an evening sun. The river. I had lost sight of it. My exhilaration at the freedom I would enjoy tomorrow ebbed with the realisation. The chains would still be attached. Real freedom was still a long way away.

'Don't look so sad,' said Li Mei, putting her arm round my shoulder. 'Tomorrow we will have fun. Don't spoil it by looking further ahead.'

I sighed, then grinned at her. 'All right, oh wise one. Race you to the shower.'

We charged down the gangway between the beds and out through the door. I reached the cubicles first, but slid on the wet floor outside and landed in a heap. Li Mei stepped over me and tried to open the cubicle door. I grabbed hold of her leg and pulled her down beside me. We sat there, in our soggy underwear, shrieking with laughter.

'You'll be all right,' said Li Mei. 'I'll make sure you're all right.'

Lazing in bed the next morning, in the euphoria of not having to get up for another half an hour, I suddenly remembered that I had no clothes to wear. All I had was my servant's uniform. I couldn't go out in that, especially not if there were going to be boys. The wild scenarios I had dreamed up about how the day would pass exploded into nothingness. I would have to stay in the dormitory on my own.

'I can't come out with you,' I said to Li Mei while we were washing our overalls.

'Why ever not?' she asked.

'I've got nothing to wear.'

Li Mei laughed. 'We all say that.'

'I mean it,' I said. 'All I have with me is my domestic's uniform.'

When she saw my face, she leapt to her feet, ran back to the dormitory and reappeared several minutes later as though nothing had happened. It wasn't until I returned to the dormitory myself, and discovered the neat pile of clothes on my bed, that I found out what she had done.

'Trousers courtesy of Dong Ying, blouse courtesy of Song Shuru, jacket courtesy of Li Mei, hair slide courtesy of Shen Enqing,' said Li Mei triumphantly.

'Try them on,' instructed Song Shuru.

'Fashion show coming up, girls,' announced Dong Ying.

I blushed shyly. 'You're so kind,' I said.

I took off my pyjamas and climbed carefully into the borrowed clothes. Although far from new, they were the prettiest clothes I had ever worn, and the most grown-up. If it hadn't been for my neatly bobbed hair and clumpy, sensible shoes, I should have felt like an empress.

'Give us a twirl, then,' said Song Shuru.

'A little bit big, but otherwise perfect,' said Li Mei.

'Now, no more talk about not going out.'

I changed into my spare overalls to help clean the dormitory, which took quite a considerable time. We had to scrub out the showers and the latrines, hang our wet overalls out to dry, change the sheets on our beds, sweep and mop the floors throughout, empty the bins, and collect up the extraordinary number of white feathers that had drifted into every corner of the room and which clung to cobwebs, curtains and bedding.

'Better make sure we don't miss any,' muttered Li Mei. 'They'll use any excuse to fine us.'

At last, at one o'clock, we were all ready. Everyone looked so much more beautiful in their normal clothes. Some of the girls had put on make-up, which made them seem very sophisticated. I was sure they wouldn't want me tagging along with them, so I kept close to Li Mei when we gradually split up into smaller groups on the way into town. It was freezing cold, a fierce wind slowing our progress as we crocodiled along the road, but we were too intent on enjoying ourselves to let it bother us.

Ahead and behind us were bunches of boys and girls from other parts of the factory. They were as happy as we were. Shouts of laughter, whistles and cheers echoed backwards and forwards. Whenever another group caught up with or overtook us, we exchanged greetings and bantered good-humouredly. I felt as though I were a member of a great big club. In my shiny red jacket, my soft black trousers, my hair blowing wildly but fashionably pinned at the back with Shen Enqing's jewel-encrusted slide, I was happier than I could remember and full of expectation.

Once we had passed the industrial outskirts of the town and numerous grimy side streets crammed with cheerless single-storey shacks, we turned a corner and the road widened into a tawdry, rackety shopping area. Multiple coloured neon lights flashed above the door-ways and in the windows of the shops and eateries, even though it was still daylight. Music blared in a riot of competing tunes from shops selling jeans, cheap silk, ice creams, mobile phones and televisions. Hairdressers had chairs set out on the pavement regardless of the cold; there were mahjong parlours, photo parlours and karaoke bars.

I was startled by the brashness of it all. The market town I had visited with my father had been colourful and bustling, the town I had visited with Mrs Chen had been sparkling and elegant. Here was something different again. The centre of this town throbbed with exuberance, in stark contrast to the grim reality of life in its factories and streets. Certainly, the workers from the factories, as soon as they reached the shopping area, became like dogs let off the leash.

'Ice cream, ice cream, give me that lovely ice cream,' chanted Dong Ying.

We piled into a shop selling ice creams in eight tempting flavours.

'I don't know which one to choose,' I said, desperate to avoid the disappointment of picking the least tasty.

'Choose more than one, then,' a boy in front turned to say. 'Who's counting?'

The thought of such extravagance made me blush, as did the mere fact of being spoken to by him, but then I saw that everyone ahead of me was coming away with three or four scoops.

'Spoil yourself,' said Dong Ying. 'You won't get many chances.'

'Not once the peak season begins,' grimaced Song Shuru.

I clutched the money that had been left in my locker. Whoever had given it to me had intended me to spend it on myself. I would start saving as soon as I received my own wages at the end of the week.

'Three scoops, please,' I said when I reached the front of the queue. 'Peach, vanilla and ginger.'

We walked slowly along the road, gazing at the clothes in the shops, licking at our ice creams, which would have tasted delicious after the food at the factory even if I hadn't made the best choice. Dong Ying darted into one shop to try on a jumper. While we waited, we browsed through the racks of blouses, skirts and trousers. Li Mei pounced on a long-sleeved yellow blouse and held it up against me.

'This was made for you, Lu Si-yan. When you earn your first wages you must come into town and buy it.'

The other girls nodded enthusiastic agreement.

I looked at myself in a mirror, astonished to see how I had changed again. I was very thin, but my eyes sparkled with excitement and my cheeks were pink from the cold wind. The yellow blouse suited me. How I wished I could buy it, but I had only just committed myself to saving as soon as I received my first wage packet. Then

168

again, I thought, I couldn't expect to borrow my friends' clothes all the time. Having a valid reason to buy the blouse made me glow with pleasure momentarily, for I had never bought any clothes for myself before. And I told myself that the blouse was so cheap that it would eat up only a tiny amount of my wages.

We strolled in and out of shops all along the road. None of us had much money to spend, but we were happy to dream and to watch other people. The long hours and the monotony of their jobs made many of the factory workers reckless and extravagant when they found themselves suddenly free to do as they liked. The shopkeepers, reliant upon these once-weekly shopping sprees to feed their families, cajoled and encouraged us through their doors in the hopes of making a sale. The result was a carnival atmosphere, exuberant and infectious.

Li Mei linked her arm through mine.

'Come on, young lady,' she grinned. 'Let's go and sing.'

She pulled me towards a karaoke bar, urged on by Dong Ying and Song Shuru.

'I can't sing,' I protested, laughing.

'Of course you can,' coaxed Li Mei. 'We'll sing together.'

'But you're too good.'

'Singing is freedom and happiness. Today you are free and happy. Sing, Lu Si-yan.'

The darkened bar was crowded with people, even though it was the middle of the afternoon. Coloured spotlights lit a small platform where a young man was crooning and gyrating to an over-loud backing track. I put my fingers in my ears. I had never seen or heard anything like it.

'Nothing could be worse than that,' shouted Shen Enqing. 'For goodness sake put him out of his misery, Li Mei.'

'As soon as he's finished then, Lu Si-yan,' yelled Li Mei.

She went over to the man in charge of the karaoke machine and whispered something in his ear. He nodded and, after a few seconds, slowly faded out the previous music. The young man leapt from the platform to mocking applause, while Li Mei pulled me up in his place. The strains of a new tune gradually became audible and I realised that it was one of my father's favourites.

'I've heard you humming it,' grinned Li Mei. 'Let's show them how it's done.'

I couldn't believe I was standing up there in front of dozens of people I didn't know. I wanted to run away and hide. My heart thumped wildly, I felt sick. But when Li Mei began to sing, I found myself joining in, at first shyly, then, as the music took over, with more and more assurance. Dong Ying, Song Shuru and Shen Enqing danced exotically in front of us. People tapped their feet, rapped on the bar, clapped their hands. Attracted by the commotion, passers-by crammed into the entrance of the bar and joined in as well. The music reached a crescendo, Li Mei turned to me, and we shouted out the last notes smiling broadly at each other. It was exhilarating, and I loved it.

When the music came to an end, the crowd clapped wildly, shouting for more. Li Mei called over to the karaoke man. The opening strains of another of my father's favourites filtered through to me above the clamour. Li Mei laughed at the expression of amazement on my face, then we began again. I poured myself into the song, recalling precious fragments from my past, cherishing my friends who were my present. And then the music changed again, to Li Mei's song. Shen Enqing stepped on to the platform to sing the harmony, and I moved aside.

As I rejoined Dong Ying and Song Shuru, I felt a hand tap me gently on the shoulder. I turned to find myself face to face with the boy from the ice-cream parlour.

'You sing so beautifully,' he said.

I blushed and looked away.

'You are so beautiful,' he said, taking me gently by the chin and turning my head back towards him. 'Come for a walk with me.'

'She's also very young,' intervened Dong Ying, 'and the only walking she'll be doing is with us.'

A sudden burst of wild applause greeted the final note of Li Mei's song. She beckoned to me to rejoin her on the platform to enjoy the praise. Dong Ying pushed me forwards, but the boy held me back.

'You don't have to do as they say,' he shouted above the noise.

'They're my friends,' I countered, tearing myself from his grasp. 'I choose to do what they say.'

'More fool you then,' he sneered, and disappeared through the crowd.

The owner was so delighted with the number of people we had attracted to his bar that he thrust some coins into Li Mei's hands and asked us to come again. We tumbled back out into the street, flushed with our success.

'You're a real star, Lu Si-yan,' said Shen Enqing. 'Where did you learn to sing like that?'

'I used to sing with my father, all the way to market and back on his rickshaw.'

'I bet he would have been proud of you just now,' smiled Song Shuru.

'I bet he would have been worried that his little swallow is growing up and attracting unwanted attention,' said Dong Ying warningly.

I followed her gaze and saw that the same boy was across the road, lounging against a shop window, watching my every move. Li Mei and Dong Ying linked their arms through mine.

'Doesn't give up, that one, does he?' said Dong Ying, as they marched me away, Song Shuru and Shen Enqing following close behind.

'Forget him,' said Li Mei. 'He can't do anything while Lu Si-yan has her bodyguards with her. Let's go and get our photo taken with the money we just earned.'

We piled into a photo parlour, made goofy smiles at the camera, stopped for chicken and noodles at a small cafe, then spent two hours in a mahjong parlour. Shen Enqing was happy just to watch, but each time it came to 'the twittering of the sparrows', the five of us collapsed into fits of giggles until we were threatened with expulsion if we didn't behave.

It was dark by the time we left, and I was yawning my head off. The girls insisted that I have one last look at 'my blouse' to keep me going through the week, we collected our photograph, which the girls gave me to put above my bed, and then we began the long walk back to our dormitory. It was bitterly cold now, the wind whipping through our scanty clothes, but we sang all the way home, and other returning groups joined in with us.

'I've had a wonderful day – thank you,' I said happily, as we walked across the factory grounds. 'I can't wait for next Sunday.'

Chapter Twenty-two
You Are Not Being Fair

There wasn't another Sunday like that first Sunday. When we were called, one by one, to collect our wages the following Friday, the news spread like wildfire that a big order had come in and that we were to work every day until it had been fulfilled, including on Sundays up until nine o'clock.

I was devastated when I heard. It was the thought of our Sunday outing that had kept me going during the week. The grinding, back-breaking monotony of sewing on ears, the supervisor's constant sniping, the foul meals, the lack of sleep – I could cope with all of them as long as there was that one day when we could go out, have fun, be ourselves, feel free. Now it was being taken from us.

'Ah well, at least we won't be tempted to spend our

hard-earned money,' sighed Li Mei, who always tried to look on the bright side.

I nodded and knew that I should have felt some relief, but I wouldn't be able to buy my blouse now. Because I had made up my mind to have it, it hit me harder that I was to be denied.

More bad news was to come. We had all had our wages docked to pay for the pillow we had torn, and a further amount had been subtracted because we had failed to pick up all the feathers.

'They could buy fifty luxury pillows with the amount they've taken from us,' fumed Dong Ying.

When it was my turn to see Mr Wang, I entered his office feeling angry and rebellious. I glared at him defiantly as I sat down, revolted by his vast paunch and a dribble of spit that clung to his chin.

'Well now, young lady, things are improving, definitely improving. Not up to scratch yet, a bit slow, but better. Just to show what a reasonable chap I am, I'm going to pay you half wages, even though you're still in training. No overtime, mind – that's only for fully-trained operatives, and there was your little bit of illness last Friday for which I've had to deduct an amount, and, as you are probably aware, I've charged you all for the wanton destruction of company property. Lastly, of course I've kept back a small sum to go towards your repayment of the ferry fare, but I'm sure you'll agree that I've been remarkably generous.'

'But you promised I'd be home for Spring Festival. I'll never have enough money if you keep taking it away,' I complained.

'No promises, dear. I said if you worked hard enough, but you're not quite up to it yet and, of course, if I keep having to deduct sums for mindless vandalism ... I should have a word with your friends about that. Now, off you go, dear, and close the door behind you.'

'You are not being fair,' I yelled at him as I stood to leave. 'You're just not being fair.'

I slammed the door behind me and stormed back along the corridor.

In the dormitory, that evening, I opened my wage packet to discover that I hadn't been paid enough money to buy my blouse, even if we were to have gone into town on the Sunday.

'How am I ever going to get home?' I cried to Li Mei. She stroked my hair, but her awkward silence smothered any lingering spark of hope.

I was constantly in trouble from that day. I struggled to keep up as the realisation that I wouldn't be home for Spring Festival, nor even for my birthday two weeks later, sank in deeper and deeper. I had been a fool even to think there was a possibility of earning enough money that quickly. I would look around at the other girls. Some of them had been there for months, even years, going home to visit periodically, but returning because there still wasn't sufficient income to keep their families in food and clothes. What was I working for, I kept wondering, if I wasn't going to be paid enough to go home and help my own family? The answer filled me with utter despair. I was there because I had no choice, and because at least, even if it took me two years, one day I would have earned enough.

But how was I to cope with two years? How was I to cope with one year, six months, three months even? The other girls managed, somehow, to keep going, to put on a brave face, to focus on some minute flicker of light at the end of an impossibly long tunnel. I was a child though, five years younger than the youngest of them. I was so physically and mentally exhausted by what I had already been through – the growing up I had already had to do, the pitfalls that seemed to lie in wait for me round every corner – that I felt I would break into a hundred pieces at the slightest touch.

My journey of a thousand miles had led me here. Was I at the end of that journey? Was I to make what I could of my life from this point onwards, and accept that I wasn't going home, that I would never see my mother and my brother again?

Chapter Twenty-three
A Gesture of Goodwill

Much to my surprise, we were allowed a day's holiday on the Sunday of Spring Festival, as well as being allowed to finish at half past six on the Saturday evening. Quite a few of the workers from the local factories went home, some of them taking extra days of unpaid leave. By then I had been paid half wages for two more weeks, but at least there had been no further unforeseen deductions.

On the Friday before Spring Festival weekend, Mr Wang called us in one by one, as usual, only to announce that wages would henceforward be paid monthly in arrears, and that the week just gone by would be included in the first month. We were to receive no money that day, nor indeed until the end of the following three weeks. The delight we all felt at the thought of a day off was immediately obliterated by the fact that some workers no longer had enough money to go home.

'They're doing it so that anyone who goes home is forced to return,' raged Dong Ying, who had herself planned to visit her parents but could now only afford the fare. 'How can I go home and eat my parents' food without contributing a penny to the cost?'

'I'm sure they would still prefer to see you,' reasoned Li Mei, 'even if you go home empty-handed. An extra mouth for two days will not make a lot of difference.'

'But I wanted to treat them. I was relying upon this week's wages to buy them something special.'

'For them, nothing will be more special than a visit from their only daughter,' Li Mei urged.

Dong Ying allowed herself to be persuaded and set off for the station in the early hours of Saturday morning. Li Mei, Song Shuru, Shen Enqing and I tried to console ourselves by making plans for our own Sunday. Everywhere in town would be closed, so we would have to entertain ourselves. Mrs Wang had announced that there would be a special feast in the canteen on Saturday, and notices went up encouraging those of us who were staying to take part in a talent show on Sunday afternoon.

My friends started to chatter about what we might do. I couldn't help feeling that all I wanted to do was to sleep the day away, so that I could block out the invading images of my mother and Li-hu at home without me. So that I wouldn't have to remember the Spring Festivals gone by, when Father was still alive; when we used to sing our way to market to sell our pig and come back laden with special treats, because Spring Festival was a time of national celebration, a time to be extravagant, a time to forget about hardship; when we used to eat and laugh and go to the village for the parade and eat and laugh some more and wait for the firecrackers at midnight; when we were so happy that nothing, nothing could burst our bubble of joy.

The determined enthusiasm of my friends wore down my resistance, and I found myself agreeing to take part in a playlet, based upon *The Bridge of Magpies*, a popular folktale, which we were going to put together on the Sunday morning. I was to play a princess, separated from her husband by the River of Stars that divides the northern skies from the southern kingdom of the heavens. Only once a year, on the seventh day of the seventh month, is she allowed to be by his side, when all the magpies on earth fly up to heaven and form a bridge over the River of Stars. Shen Enqing was to be the prince, Song Shuru the king, and Li Mei the narrator.

After we had finished work on Saturday, we headed back to the dormitory, each of us full of our own far-away thoughts, but all of us wanting to be family to each other.

'We may not be able to be at home with our families, but I'd rather be here with my friends than anywhere else,' said Li Mei, voicing how we all felt.

We were surprised to find brightly coloured cut-outs of fish and birds hanging from the door and windows.

'They *are* making an effort,' said Shen Enqing sarcastically.

'Probably paid for with our wages,' grimaced Song Shuru.

'Take it as a gesture of goodwill,' said Li Mei, 'or we'll make ourselves miserable, and I for one don't want to be miserable. Not tonight. Not tomorrow.'

We changed for dinner, dressing ourselves up as though we were going out somewhere special. Dong

Ying had left a spare pair of trousers and a blouse for me to wear, and Shen Enqing lent me her jewel-encrusted slide. Song Shuru insisted that I put on some lipstick.

'You're going to be twelve in two weeks' time. Feel what it's like to be a woman for one evening. Prepare for your metamorphosis into a princess tomorrow.'

She painted my lips and held a mirror in front of me. I was shocked by the transformation. It was extraordinary how a little smudge of red could add years to my age.

'Give us a pout,' said Shen Enqing.

I puckered my lips and we dissolved with laughter.

'You'll do,' chuckled Li Mei. 'Come on, let's have fun.'

We did have fun. The workers who had stayed behind and who normally used the other canteen were to use our canteen that weekend, adding to the noisy air of festivity. The canteen ceiling had been decorated with huge red lanterns, the tables were covered with red cloths, and large, colourful fish, birds and animals made of paper covered the walls. Everyone had dressed up and a party atmosphere was evident the minute we entered the room. A table at the front of the room was covered with a gold cloth and had two white ibises carved from turnips as a centrepiece.

'Looks like we've got special guests,' said Shen Enqing, admiring the centrepiece, which was beautiful.

'There's nothing special about the Wangs,' said Song Shuru.

She shut up quickly when Li Mei prodded her in the back and nodded towards the door. Mr Wang entered and waddled self-importantly across the room, followed by Mrs Wang, mincing in his wake, followed by his strutting managers and supervisors. We waited for a cue from him, then took our places at our own tables. Waiters immediately danced attention upon the top-table guests, serving each with sweet red wine. Large bottles of beer were placed on our tables. This was the first time we had ever been allowed alcohol. The bottles were passed round quickly, everyone eager to make the most of this rare treat from the Wangs. Mr Wang raised a first toast, to the health of his company.

'Just sip, Lu Si-yan,' warned Li Mei. 'There could be many toasts and you will be expected to join in with them all.'

I did as she said, which wasn't difficult because I had

no taste for the bitter, pale amber liquid before me. Then the food began to arrive. Enormous platters of chicken, beef, duck, fish and dumplings were carried ceremoniously to the top table. The dishes deposited on our tables were smaller and less varied, but still the food was delicious compared with our normal fare. Stiff and restricted at first by the presence of the Wangs, the workers gradually relaxed and the noise levels rose again. Conversations grew louder and more ribald amongst the males, and the girls grew giggly under the influence of the beer. The toasts came thick and fast: to the kindness of the factory owner; to the good fortune of the workers to be in his employ; to the health and wealth of the factory owner and his wife; to an increase in orders; to an increase in profits.

Shen Enqing, giggly herself by now, leant over to me and raised her glass. 'May he slip on a banana skin,' she chuckled. 'May he choke on his own self-importance.'

I raised my own glass to that, and drank deeply, spluttering as the bubbles caught the back of my throat. I lowered the glass and felt a hand on my shoulder. A head pressed against mine and a voice whispered, 'Are you still doing what they say?'

I turned to see the boy from the karaoke bar disappearing towards a table at the back of the room. I was so shocked that the colour must have drained from my face.

'You look as if you've seen a ghost,' chuckled Song Shuru. 'Is it the beer doing that?'

I tried to shrug it off. So what if he was there? So what if that meant that he worked in one of the factories? What could he do? I was with friends. They would look after me. But I couldn't help glancing round every so often to make sure that he was still at his table, worried that he might approach me again. I lost my appetite for the delicious food, and the cheerful buffoonery of the evening failed now to embrace me.

Li Mei put her hand over mine. 'Too many sips?' she smiled at me. 'Or too many sad thoughts?'

I didn't have to answer. Mr Wang banged on the table for attention and rose to make a speech. I heard little of it, except to register that it was largely self-congratulatory but contained one small word of thanks to us, his workers, before ending with a final toast to himself and his wife for hosting such a magnificent Spring Festival celebration.

We left the canteen arm in arm to the sounds of fire-crackers ringing in our ears from all over the town and the nearby countryside. The New Year had begun. I had been away from home for seven long months.

We slept late into the following morning, blissful in the knowledge that our time was our own. When, finally, we roused ourselves, slowly, delicately, the talk in the dormitory moved from the unexpected extravagance of the Wangs in providing the previous night's banquet, to their extraordinary arrogance, to the talent show and what a cheap way it was of keeping us entertained. We didn't mind. It was fun finding out who was going to do what and hearing them practise. Li Mei took us outside to run through *The Bridge of Magpies*. It was cold but bearable, though a shadow from the previous evening drifted across my mind and made me shiver.

'Our little princess will freeze waiting for her prince,' smiled Song Shuru.

We stopped at lunchtime and headed for the canteen, where the decorations were still hanging, but the food had reverted to normal.

On our way back to the dormitory to ready ourselves for our afternoon performance, a sullen-faced girl called

188

Zheng Yi grabbed my arm and spat in my ear, 'Keep away from my boyfriend, kid, or I'll make you very sorry.'

She pushed her way past me and into the dormitory before I could say a word. I couldn't have said anything anyway. I was too dumbfounded. What boyfriend? She could only have meant my tormentor from the karaoke bar, but I had done nothing to encourage him. She must have seen him approach me last night, but I hadn't encouraged that either. I hesitated outside, no longer wanting to go in, until Li Mei came to find me to begin my transformation into a princess.

I sat on my bed while Shen Enqing applied my make-up. I kept my eyes averted from the corner of the room where Zheng Yi had her bed, but I felt her watching me, hating me. When I stood to change my clothes, I caught sight of her whispering to her friends, pointing to me. Suddenly the dormitory was no longer a safe haven.

I wished now I didn't have to perform at the talent show, but I went along so as not to disappoint my friends. The tables had been removed from the canteen and a makeshift platform erected at one end of the room. Our supervisor was in charge of the running order and told us we would be the fifth to go on. We sat near the back to watch the other acts – a dance with ribbons, a singing duet, a man on a flute, a plate spinner (not very successful). Everyone cheered enthusiastically as each act ended.

Then it was our turn. We made our way to the platform and, as I turned to face the audience, I saw him. Right in the front row, staring at me. Next to him was Zheng Yi, who was watching his every move. I wanted to run away there and then, and when it came to the part in our play where the princess cries at having to leave her prince for another whole year, I cried for real and wished I could throw myself into the River of Stars and disappear for ever.

As soon as we had finished, I leapt from the platform and ran to the door. I wasn't quick enough. Zheng Yi followed and caught up with me outside. She grabbed me by the hair and pulled me round the back of the canteen.

'I told you to keep away from him,' she screamed. 'I saw you looking him up and down. I saw you giving him the come-on with those crocodile tears. I ought to kill you.'

'Please, let go, Zheng Yi,' I pleaded. 'You're wrong. I haven't done anything. I promise.'

'You must think I'm stupid,' she snarled, tugging my hair again so that my head lurched backwards. 'What are you doing here, anyway? Spilled water, are you? Mummy didn't want you? Pity she didn't flush you clean away.'

She pushed me to the ground and stood above me.

'You might think life is difficult enough here already, but I can make it even more difficult. Believe me. This is just the start.'

Chapter Twenty-four
Ready to Run

She was right. Two weeks later, on my birthday, I was removed from my job.

I woke in the morning to find a cluster of little gifts by my bedside: a hairslide from Dong Ying, a book from Li Mei, a silk bag from Shen Enqing and an exquisite hand-made card from Song Shuru. Apart from the card, the presents were all personal possessions which my friends had chosen to give to me. I was greatly touched by their kindness, and hugged them one by one.

'Twelve years old, eh?' said Dong Ying. 'You'll soon be a grown-up.'

I aimed a playful punch at her, and as I did, I caught sight of Zheng Yi standing in the corner of the room looking at me smugly.

'A very happy birthday, Lu Si-yan,' she mouthed,

before turning to her friends to begin a whispering session.

'What's going on between you and Zheng Yi?' asked Li Mei, who had picked up on the unease I felt in her presence.

'I don't think she likes me very much, that's all,' I replied. I had no wish to escalate the problem by involving my friends.

'Probably because you're prettier than her,' said Dong Ying. 'She's always been a sourpuss that one, anyway. Come on then, girls, let's go and stuff those bears.'

We skipped across the yard arm in arm, laughing at our own silliness, and tumbled through the factory door.

'Eyes, here we come,' said Li Mei and marched off to her bench.

'Ears, here we come,' I copied.

But as soon as I reached my bench the supervisor called me over to speak to me. She said that she had received several complaints that I was too slow, that I was holding up the production line. She said that she herself had always felt that I wasn't up to the job. I was to work instead as a 'runner' in the factory next door. It had been decided. Mr Wang was aware of the situation.

I was to have no say in the matter. I was to start straight-away that morning. Li Mei and my friends tried to argue on my behalf, but with no success.

I was numb with shock when the supervisor led me out into the cold February air, across the concrete yard and through the doors into my new workplace. The blast of sweat, heat and noxious fumes that greeted me as we entered made me feel sick on the spot. The noise from the rows of machines was pulverising.

I looked anxiously across the room. Most of the work-ers in this factory were men. Some of them eyed me up and down with disdain, others with curiosity, one or two flirtatiously. I lowered my eyes, horrified, and waited to be told what to do.

The supervisor in this factory, a small man with a wizened face and rat-like eyes, showed me round.

'Your job,' he said, 'is to make sure there are no hold-ups in production. As each worker on the line completes a particular task, you must race, race, race whatever part of the toy they have been working on to the next person in the line. You must watch, watch, watch, so that you're ready to run.'

He showed me the order in which the production line

operated, and a sample of the toy currently being made – a large multicoloured plastic dumper truck. Li-hu would have adored it.

'Things are fairly quiet here at the moment,' the supervisor continued, 'but in a month or so's time we'll be at full stretch. Are you ready to race, girl, are you ready to run?'

I suddenly felt a strong desire to laugh out loud as I pictured this funny little man turning into a rat and scuttling into a hole. I took a deep breath and nodded.

'Good girl, good. Off you go then, and remember to watch, watch, watch.'

There were thirteen machines in operation at that moment, though there were double that number in the building. I started circling round them, trying to fathom out the best way to see as many operators as possible at a time. Some of the processes took longer than others, so the order of completion of tasks was totally random. It was a case of reacting as soon as a worker put his part of the truck down, grabbing it and taking it to the next machine.

The speed at which the tasks were achieved was breathtaking. I had thought I would be able to sit down regularly, but no sooner had I picked up and run from one worker to the next than another one was ready and waiting. The supervisor, much quicker to spot a completed task or a worker twiddling his thumbs than I was, was equally quick to shout at me to keep up. In the rank, airless atmosphere, I found it difficult to breathe, could feel myself wilting, but I dared not stop. I had no doubt that if I failed again to make the grade, I would be dismissed on the spot. I had survived for seven weeks. Mr Wang owed me nearly four weeks' more money. I had made a start on saving to go home. I remembered dear Mrs Hong's words: 'Your resilience will see you through'. I wasn't going to fail now, not if I could help it.

I was comforted to rediscover my friends in the canteen at lunchtime. They bombarded me with questions about my new job. When I told them about Mr Ratty Eyes and his 'watch, watch, watch, run, run, run', they hooted with derision. 'Are you ready to race, girl, are you ready to run?' became our catchphrase, and was greeted with howls of laughter every time we used it. My friends were shocked to learn that I hadn't been allowed to sit down all morning, and that one of the men put his hand on mine every time I went near him.

'Smack him on the head with his toy part, that's what I would do,' raged Dong Ying.

'Drive a dumper truck over his fingers,' offered Song Shuru. 'You poor thing. What a way to spend your twelfth birthday.'

I nodded glumly. 'It's awful, truly awful. The only good thing is that we finish at half past ten, at the moment at least.'

'Now that *is* good,' smiled Li Mei. 'You'll have had an hour and a half's sleep before we come stampeding in to wake you up again.'

'I'd rather be with you and the bears for an extra hour and a half than with Ratty Eyes and Groper,' I grimaced.

I really didn't know how I managed to stay on my feet for the rest of that day. Even standing up after dinner was difficult enough, and I still had another three and a half hours to go. The relief I felt when at last I returned to the dormitory that evening, and the pleasure I felt at having it all to myself, were indescribable. I threw myself on to my bed, stared mindlessly at the ceiling for a few minutes, then fell asleep.

When I woke again, I was still alone. I went for a shower and stayed under for an eternity, almost as though I could wash away the horrors of the day. Afterwards, I sprawled on the bed, luxuriating in my cleanness, and picked up the book Li Mei had given me. I couldn't concentrate, though. The words danced up and down in front of my eyes and made no sense, for part of me was listening for the sounds of the other girls returning.

I had fallen into a doze when the door clattered open. Zheng Yi and her cronies came in first – deliberately, I suspected. She quickly approached my bed and said, smugly, 'I hope you've had a nice birthday, Lu Si-yan.'

I turned away from her. She grabbed my hair and pulled me back.

'Don't turn your back on me when I'm talking to you, Lu Si-yan. Where are your manners? No wonder your mother got rid of you.'

That was enough. I kicked out at her as hard as I could, caught her in the stomach, and sent her flailing on to the floor between the beds. She scrambled to her feet, urged on by her cronies, and was about to aim a punch at my face, when Li Mei and my other friends came through the door and yelled at her to stop.

'You keep your snotty noses out of this,' snarled

Zheng Yi. 'She started it and I'm going to finish it.'

'Leave her alone, Zheng Yi,' ordered Li Mei. 'She's done nothing to harm you.'

'And what would you know, Miss Let's-keep-it-all-sweet-and-nice?' Zheng Yi retorted.

'She's just a kid,' stepped in Dong Ying. 'Why don't you pick on someone your own size?'

'Who asked for your input, big mouth? She tried to steal my boyfriend. She deserves what she gets.'

I couldn't take any more. I leapt to my feet and yelled, 'I didn't do anything and you know it. You're making it all up. Why can't you just leave me alone? Haven't you caused me enough trouble?'

I flew across the room, out through the door and across the yard. It was freezing cold and I was in my nightwear, but I didn't care. I slumped down behind one of the other dormitories and prayed that no one would find me. I decided in that moment that I would have to leave. I just couldn't bear it any longer. I would wait until the end of the week, take my wages from Mr Wang, then go. I wouldn't be able to go home, I knew that, because even if I had enough to pay my fare, I certainly wouldn't have money left to give to my mother. But anything was better than the nightmare I was living now.

My teeth began to chatter as the cold nipped at my skin and bit through my clothes. I wished I had thought to grab a blanket on my way out. I could hear voices coming from the dormitory, men's voices, then other voices, girls' voices, drawing closer, moving away, then drawing closer again. I pressed myself flat against the wall, but Li Mei and Dong Ying came round the corner of the building and spotted me.

'You'll catch your death of cold out here,' said Li Mei gently.

'I don't care,' I replied. 'I'm not going back in.'

'It's all right now,' said Dong Ying. 'She won't give you any more trouble. She won't dare.'

'She doesn't need to. She's already made it impossible for me to stay here.'

'If you don't stay, then you must go home,' said Li Mei.

'You know I can't go home,' I replied.

'And you can't go and live on the streets either,' countered Dong Ying. 'You'd be prey to worse than the likes of Mr Wang.'

'There are other factories,' I tried to argue, though I knew I was losing.

'What makes you think they'll be any better?' Dong Ying persisted. 'Besides, no factory owner who obeys the law will employ a twelve-year-old.'

'You have friends here,' said Li Mei, putting her arm round my shoulder. 'Good friends who care about you. However hard everything else may seem, at least you have that. We'll do everything we can to help you, so that one day you will be able to go home.'

I knew, of course, that she was right and that I had no choice. They helped me to my feet and back to the dormitory. I went straight to my bed, pulled the blanket over me and lay there shivering, but I had noticed, as I crossed the room, that Zheng Yi was sitting on her bed in the corner with a split lip and a reddened face.

Chapter Twenty-five
All Too Much

I tried to persuade Mr Wang to let me go back to the bear factory, pleading that the work as a runner was too tiring for me, but that I was sure I would be good at stitching bears' noses, or sewing the pads on their paws.

'I'm afraid that there are no vacancies in noses and paws, my dear,' he said, without even stopping to consider my request, when I went for my wages two days after starting in my new position. 'Noses and paws are very popular, so I couldn't possibly give them to a newcomer. It would cause discontent amongst my staff, do you see, and I wouldn't want that, would I? A fit little thing like you should have no problem keeping up as a runner. In fact, I'd say the job is tailor-made for you, tailor-made. And since there has been no training involved – anyone could do it – I can pay you the full amount for the job straightaway, lucky you. Of course, there are some small deductions to help pay for the New Year celebrations, and there's still some to come off for the fare –'

'Please, Mr Wang, please let me go back with my friends,' I begged.

'As I was saying, I think you'll find I've been remarkably generous as usual. Now, off you go, dear, back to work. You can do it. I have complete faith in my choice of workers.'

The receipt of a month's wages all in one go, even though they had been severely trimmed, cheered me a little, for it seemed such an enormous amount of money. I counted the notes several times, struggling to take in the fact that they belonged to me. I wrapped them carefully inside my old blouse and pushed it to the back of my locker. I couldn't wait to add to them, for suddenly the dream of going home one day became more of a reality.

My work as a runner, though, was punishing, and was about to worsen. Two and a half weeks after I had moved jobs, a huge order came in for a range of toy farm vehicles. Suddenly, all twenty-six machines were in operation, a new group of workers was brought in, including a second runner to help me, and our hours were extended. The delicious time of solitude and relaxation I had looked forward to every evening since beginning work as a runner was snatched away from me. Our overtime was extended to midnight.

If I had thought the pace of work was breathtaking before, now it was overwhelming. It was almost impossible to keep up with the rate at which tasks were being completed, and the supervisor shouted at us constantly. The noise from the machines was mind-numbing, the heat debilitating. There was no air-conditioning in the factory, the windows were tiny, and the temperature outside was rising steadily. The air inside was stale and cloudy with fumes, which stung my eyes and made it difficult to breathe. My legs ached and my feet, already pinched raw by my too-small sensible shoes, swelled and protested at every step I took. The runner who was recruited to help me lasted for two weeks, then disappeared and didn't return. A young man was hired in her place. He had only been there a day when he complained to the supervisor that four people should be doing our job, not two. Nothing changed, and he left to be replaced by a man who seemed to delight in making me look slow. I asked again to be moved, but Mr Wang refused and told me I had better hand in my notice if I wasn't happy. He didn't want me poisoning the rest of the staff.

I didn't leave, but soon afterwards I developed a wheezy cough. It kept me awake at night, and during the day I felt as though I would pass out if I couldn't take more oxygen into my lungs. Li Mei said it must be the fibres and chemicals in the air. She went to see Mr Wang on my behalf, but he turned nasty and said that if she interfered again he would dismiss both of us on the spot and we would not be paid.

March turned to April and the outside temperature soared. Inside the factory, it was like a furnace. More orders came in. Our early finish on Sundays was taken away from us, and twice a week we had to work through until two o'clock in the morning. The atmosphere of discontent that reigned was almost as suffocating as the heat. Those workers who had some choice in the matter soon departed. Those who, like myself, had little choice, had to put up with whatever Mr Wang dictated.

My cough grew worse. I spent my days feeling

nauseous and faint. It didn't matter how much the supervisor shouted at me now, I couldn't have responded. I grew ever more fearful that I would be thrown out. My friends became increasingly concerned about my health.

One day, I was simply unable to get up in the morning.

'You must stay in bed today,' Li Mei insisted. 'They will have to manage without you.'

I hadn't the strength to argue. I slept all day long, right the way through till the next morning, waking only to eat a bowl of rice Li Mei had brought for me. I felt better for the rest, but my recovery was short-lived. A few days later I began to cough up blood. I was too terrified of what might happen to me to tell anyone. I worked on for another week, until, one afternoon, I collapsed on to the factory floor.

I was carried back to the dormitory by two of the men. Li Mei was assigned to keep an eye on me, with strict instructions to return to work as soon as I revived. She sat stroking my hand and wiping my forehead with a damp towel. I remembered my mother when she had been ill, lying so still that it was as if she were dead.

Mother had recovered, but her life had failed her. If that was the fate that awaited me, if I was doomed forever to a future as bleak as the past ten months, then I had no wish to recover. I couldn't go on. I had tried, but my best had never been good enough, and the struggle was just too great. 'You are like a fragile reed,' Mrs Chen had said. 'One puff of wind and you will break in two.' I was broken now.

I was racked by a sudden fit of coughing. As soon as Li Mei saw the blood on my pillow she ran for help. She returned with Mrs Wang, who immediately fussed around like a solicitous mother hen, while Li Mei watched her in disbelief.

'The poor girl,' she clucked. 'I always sensed that she was a sickly child, all that fainting for no reason, but she was so desperate for a job that I ignored my better instincts.' She stopped to pat my hand, but continued addressing Li Mei as though I were not there. 'How cruel of her parents to send her off to work when she's such a weak little thing. So small for her age, too. I always wondered whether she was really fifteen like she said.' She looked at me accusingly at that point, then continued, 'She must go to hospital, of course, and being good employers we'll pay, but I fear she won't be able to return here when she's better. It'll all be too much for her again. All too much.'

She ran to call an ambulance, muttering 'Poor thing, poor thing' as she left the room. Li Mei held my hand once more. Despite feeling wretched, I began to giggle. Li Mei joined in.

'That's put the cat among the pigeons,' she said. 'The last thing the Wangs want is someone asking questions about their working practices and how you came to be in this state.'

'I've always been a sickly child, didn't you realise that?' I said.

Exhaustion took over again then, and I fell into a deep sleep. I scarcely stirred as they lifted me from my bed and into the ambulance, nor during the long journey to hospital. When I arrived, I was aware of a lot of activity around me: nurses taking my temperature and putting needles into my arms, doctors examining me, disturbing me, asking questions, making notes. I didn't want to be disturbed, didn't want to wake up. I was happy handing the burden of my life to someone else.

Chapter Twenty-six
A Voice So Strange and Quiet

I drifted in and out of sleep for what seemed like days after that. Shadowy figures hovered on the fringes of my consciousness each time I came to, only to disappear again before I could identify them. I feared that one of them was Mrs Chen, another Yimou, another Zheng Yi. I seemed to have lost my ability to decipher what was real and what was imaginary. When Uncle appeared fleetingly from nowhere, I screamed until my cough took my breath, then I flailed my arms around to keep him away. Behind him, my mother clawed the air as though trying to pull me towards her. Even when Uncle seemed to have gone, Mother stayed there reaching out to me, but I couldn't run to her, couldn't run to her. Uncle's tight grip around my wrist was holding me back. I screamed at him to let go, kicked out at his invisible presence, and when at last he did let go, I fell back into a bottomless sleep.

I woke at last, late one morning, to dazzling sunlight spilling across my bed from a window opposite. Through the window I could see that the sun was high in a pale blue sky feathered with clouds. I blinked in confusion, trying to remember where I was, who I was.

Little by little, my shadow world fell away as other beds came into focus and uniformed figures bustled to and fro between them. I had no idea how long I had been there, and I was too weak to move, but I felt somehow safe and would have been happy just to lie there for ever and watch.

A small movement to my left made me turn my head. A man was sitting by the side of the bed, head bowed, hands clasped, as though lost in contemplation. He became aware of my gaze and looked up. The minute he did, I turned away. It was Uncle Ba. I wasn't safe. The nightmare wasn't over.

How long had he been there? How had he found me?

What did he want?

I heard him stand up and clear his throat. I waited for the usual words of criticism, words of scorn, knowing that after what I had been through they would have no power to touch me.

'How are you feeling, Si-yan?' Uncle said at last, in a voice so strange and quiet that I almost thought it had come from someone else. The question hung tantalisingly in the air. How did he expect me to feel? I lay there motionless, the fraught silence begging me to have my say, but no words found their way out. I sensed Uncle shifting uneasily. Let him suffer.

'I have come to take you home, Si-yan.'

My heart skipped. More silence.

'I have been trying to find you these last four months. There was a letter from Mrs Chen's mother-in-law to your mother saying that you were on your way home. But you never arrived. And then, when I tried to retrace your steps, it was as though you had disappeared.'

I might as well have done, Uncle Ba, for all you cared.

'I have travelled a thousand miles to find you, Si-yan. I had all but given up when the hospital made contact.'

Why so much effort, Uncle Ba? I turned towards him.

He looked shrunken somehow, and haggard. He avoided my gaze and sat back down in the chair. Then he leant forward and tried to take my hand. I pulled it away sharply. How dared he?

'Si-yan,' he said. 'There is something I have to tell you.' His voice quavered in its reluctance to speak. 'Si-yan –' he said, and paused again.

I stared at him and despised his sudden weakness.

'It's your mother, Si-yan.'

The air grew taut.

'What about my mother?' My own voice frightened me. 'Where is my mother?' I tried to sit up, wanting to challenge the man I hated to say anything against her.

'Your mother is dead.'

The words struck me like daggers, though they were spoken in the smallest whisper. I screamed then, over and over again, ripping the air into shreds. Uncle tried to calm me, but I hit him with all my might.

'She's not dead, she's not dead! How can she be? Why are you saying such things? I hate you, I hate you, I hate you!' I screamed.

Nurses came running, I heard Li Mei's voice. Nothing could stop me, though. My pain was devouring

212

every ounce of my body and threatening everyone else around me. I fought against the comforting words and restraining hands, fought against the efforts to make things better. They couldn't be made better. It was Mother's job to make things better, and she had gone.

I screamed until my cough robbed me of my breath and I succumbed to a drug-induced sleep.

Li Mei was sitting by my bed when I woke again. The news of my mother assaulted me afresh and I began to sob.

'Tell me it's not true, please tell me it's not true.'

Li Mei held me tight, quietly stroked my hair, and her silence told me again what I didn't want to believe.

'Where's Uncle?' I asked at last.

'He's asleep on a bench outside.'

'It's his fault, Li Mei, I know it's his fault.'

'He says it was pneumonia, that your mother was too weak to fight it,' Li Mei said gently.

'Too weak because of him,' I countered.

'He blames himself terribly, Si-yan.'

'Am I supposed to feel sorry for him?' I howled. 'He sold me, Li Mei, sold me like a bucket of pakchoi, just because we owed him money. All he ever thinks about is money. And now he's killed my mother because of his meanness.'

Li Mei held my hand. 'He wants to make amends, Lu Si-yan. The way he treated you can never be excused, but there are things he has told me that you may not know.'

I looked at her angrily. 'What sort of things? He's just trying to get you on his side, Li Mei. You don't know him like I do. He's always been mean, always selfish, always finding fault when we were doing our best. Father loved him, but all Uncle could do was criticise him. And he's always hated me. Always, always, always.'

She told me, then, what she had learned from Uncle while I was asleep. I knew already that Uncle had helped to bring up my father after the death of their parents. I didn't know quite how bitter that had made him at the loss of his own childhood. I didn't know that even when Uncle was a simple farmer, he had helped Father to establish his own farm. I didn't know, and neither did my mother, that when I was born, by which time Uncle was working in a factory, he had made payments to my father whenever times were hard. When Li-hu was born, Uncle had at last seen a time in the future when he would no longer have any responsibility for us. Li-hu and Father would share that responsibility. Then Father had died, and suddenly he was more responsible than ever.

'When your father died,' Li Mei continued, 'your uncle supported your mother more and more, but he became increasingly embittered. You bore the brunt of his bitterness because, like many men of his generation, he considered you good for marriage and little else.'

'But I tried so hard,' I protested.

'It wouldn't have mattered how hard you tried. It wouldn't have made any difference once he had made up his mind to reduce his burden by settling your future elsewhere.'

'By selling me, you mean.'

'He says he chose your future in-laws very carefully.'

'Not carefully enough,' I snapped. 'I'm sure he just sold me to the highest bidder. Nothing matters to Uncle except money.'

'He is paying a terrible price now for his actions. He has seen what harm it caused to your mother and to you. He has to live with the knowledge that he allowed his own bitterness to split his family apart.'

215

'Let him pay the price then, why should I care?' I sobbed. 'He took my mother from me, and I'll never forgive him.'

'He needs you, Si-yan, and so does your brother.'

'I am just a girl-child,' I said bitterly. 'How can he possibly need me, except to cook his meals and run errands for him? Don't you see, Li Mei? We're more of a burden than ever now.'

'You and your brother are all the family your uncle has left. Go home and give him a chance, Si-yan.'

The emptiness I felt inside was worse than the pain I had endured before. I had nothing to look forward to any more. My survival over the past few months had been built upon the belief that, one day, I would go home and be with my mother. What was there now? I wandered back through the paths of my childhood, tried to grasp hold of the happy times and not let them go. There was Father singing in his rickshaw, bumping his way to market; Mother sitting on the river bank laughing with the other village women; Li-hu chasing hens and yelling with delight every time he found an egg. Little Li-hu, my apple-cheeked baby brother. Nearly a year had gone by since I had left him behind in my mother's arms. He would have grown. I might not even recognise him. Would he know me? How was he coping without Mother?

Suddenly, more than anything in the world, I wanted to be with him, wanted to hold him, wanted to make things better for him, wanted to take away his pain, wanted to tell him that I loved him. 'When he is old enough, my handsome tiger will protect and treasure my beautiful silk swallow,' my father had said. But he wasn't old enough. He was only six. 'Perhaps your silk swallow will protect and treasure your handsome tiger,' I had laughingly replied. Well, I would protect him. I would be mother and father and sister to him. And I wouldn't resent it. Not for one moment.

'I want to be with my brother,' I said.

Li Mei squeezed my hand and left the room. She returned with Uncle, who hovered by the door, all his self-assurance gone. I noticed the dark circles under his eyes before I turned my head away, unable to cope with his uneasiness on top of my grief. He stepped forward and spoke.

'I am not asking you to forgive me, Si-yan, just for a chance to repair some of the damage I have done. My selfishness has nearly destroyed this family, I see that now. I want to give you and your brother a home. I don't want you to be a mother to Li-hu, it is too much to ask of any child. I want you to go back to school, Si-yan, to make something of yourself. Li-hu too.'

I looked at him. Did he really mean it? Had he changed so much? I had changed, I knew that.

'I am not the child you sent away ten months ago, Uncle. I will come home with you for the sake of my brother, and for the sake of my mother and father. But I cannot forgive you, and I will not be your servant.'

Uncle nodded. 'You have come a long way,' he said, 'and so have I.'

Chapter Twenty-seven

Let it Be Somewhere Better

It was another week before I was strong enough to leave hospital. Uncle came to see me every day. We were so awkward together at first that I almost dreaded his visits. He tried hard to make things right between us. They couldn't be, though, not just like that, not for a very long time.

Uncle talked frankly about Mother and how, when she had fallen ill, she had begged him to find me and bring me home. A letter had come from Mrs Hong saying that I was on my way, but when I hadn't arrived Mother's condition had worsened. Uncle had set out to look for me, but had been called back as my mother's life failed her.

He talked about Li-hu, how he had grown, and how much he looked like our father. I could see that Uncle adored my brother, that my brother had unlocked his heart. I doubted Uncle would ever feel like that about me, and feared that it would only ever be guilt that made him accept me back.

Mostly, I just listened. I grasped at little bits of information that helped me to build pictures of my mother and Li-hu at home without me: Uncle playing with Li-hu; Mother struggling to cope; Mother lying ill; my brother without Mother at home with Uncle. They were uncomfortable pictures, but I needed to see them. I watched for signs that would show the old Uncle was still only just below the surface, ready to re-emerge. I studied him hard, trying to work out whether or not his regret was honest. Part of me wanted to believe it because, apart from Li-hu, Uncle was the only family I had left. The other part of me fought against such belief, because I wasn't ready to take his side.

Li Mei disappeared during that week, saying that she had something to sort out and that she would visit again before I left. She returned one afternoon with a big smile on her face and clutching a brown envelope.

'This is for you,' she said triumphantly.

'What is it?'

'Open it and see.'

I unsealed the envelope and pulled out a wad of notes.

'It's the money the Wangs owed you, and I managed to extract some extra,' she grinned. 'They were worried that your uncle might report them for employing underage children and other illegal working practices. Mr Wang was extremely friendly and very happy to pay you what I demanded.'

I laughed at the thought of the obnoxious Mr Wang humbly doing what Li Mei told him.

'Will you go back?' I wanted to know.

'I don't think they'd have me, somehow,' chuckled Li Mei, 'but with the extra that Mr Wang insisted I too deserved, I'm going home as well, Lu Si-yan, and then I shall find work somewhere else.'

'Somewhere better,' I said. 'Let it be somewhere better.'

Chapter Twenty-eight
Fragments of a Song

As soon as I was well enough to travel, we began the long journey home. Uncle called a taxi early one afternoon and helped me into the back. Li Mei sat alongside me, her own journey home taking her part of the way with us. I soon fell asleep, my head bouncing up and down on her shoulder. I woke when we came to a halt. It was dark outside, but I could hear the eerie sounds of distant engines and horns.

We had come to a river. A huge ferry was moored at the end of a jetty. Men with wicker baskets on their backs were walking down to it, bent double under the weight of oranges and vegetables. Others had long poles slung across their shoulders, at the ends of which were buckets full of fish. Two men were pushing a cart piled high with meat.

'Are we going on that enormous ferry?' I asked.

'For the next two days and five hundred miles,' said Uncle.

Uncle carried me aboard. I was still too weak to walk very far. He took me to the cabin I was to share with Li Mei, settled me on one of the beds, then left us to go and find something to drink. I pulled back the curtains to look at the river, but all I could see was the dappling of reflected light across a blanket of black. I turned to Li Mei.

'While I have been away, I have believed that as long as I could see the river, any river, one day it would take me home. Yet so often it has disappeared from sight or been shrouded in black. Now, at last, the river is taking me home, but still it is hidden from me, and my dream has been smashed.'

I began to weep and Li Mei rushed to my side. There was nothing she could say, but her presence was a comfort and I was so happy to have her with me for a little while longer.

After we had eaten, we both fell asleep. I woke the next morning alone in the cabin. I had no idea what time it was, but from the noise of the engines I could tell that we were moving. Sunlight was smouldering through the curtains. I opened them on to a pure blue sky. I gazed in fascination as the river bustled by, sparkling and frolicsome. Another ferry drew level with us and its passengers waved. I waved back until I could no longer see them. I made up my mind then to dress and go up on deck.

It took all my willpower to climb the steps and make my way to the front of the ship. Ahead of me, Li Mei was facing forwards, leaning against the railings, the wind streaming through her hair. The wind carried fragments of a song, which knitted together as I drew closer. It was Li Mei's song, her beautiful song about mist and mountains, rivers and waterfalls, a cormorant fisherman sailing quietly along in the golden light of an evening sun. I stood by her side and began to sing with her. Then, as I looked all around me, I saw Uncle on the deck below brushing a tear from his eyes.

'The journey of a thousand miles starts from beneath your feet' was one of my father's favourite sayings. Where was I now on my journey? Or was this a new journey about to begin?